ADENELA
She doesn't look like a deity, but she's the Goddess of War. She teaches Seiya swordsmanship.

SEIYA RYUUGUUIN
The overly cautious Hero summoned by Rista.

MASH
A dragonkin warrior. Seiya's bag carrier no. 1.

ARIADOA
A seasoned goddess and Rista's mentor.

7/2019

THE HERO IS OVERPOWERED BUT OVERLY CAUTIOUS

STORY **LIGHT TUCHIHI**

ILLUS. **SAORI TOYOTA**

1

YEN ON

NEW YORK

THE HERO IS OVERPOWERED BUT OVERLY CAUTIOUS 1

LIGHT TUCHIHI

Translation by Matt Rutsohn
Cover art by Saori Toyota

KONO YUSHA GA ORE TUEEE KUSENI SHINCHO SUGIRU Vol. 1
©Light Tuchihi, Saori Toyota 2017
First published in Japan in 2017 by KADOKAWA CORPORATION, Tokyo.
English translation rights arranged with KADOKAWA CORPORATION, Tokyo through
TUTTLE-MORI AGENCY, INC., Tokyo.

English translation © 2019 by Yen Press, LLC

Yen On
1290 Avenue of the Americas
New York, NY 10104

Visit us at yenpress.com • facebook.com/yenpress • twitter.com/yenpress • yenpress.tumblr.com
instagram.com/yenpress

First Yen On Edition: June 2019

Yen On is an imprint of Yen Press, LLC.
The Yen On name and logo are trademarks of Yen Press, LLC.

Library of Congress Cataloging-in-Publication Data
Names: Tuchihi, Light, author. I Toyota, Saori, illustrator. I Rutsohn, Matt, translator.
Title: The hero is overpowered but overly cautious / Light Tuchihi ;
illustration by Saori Toyota ; translation by Matt Rutsohn ; cover art by Saori Toyota.
Other titles: Kono yusha ga ore tueee kuseni shinchou sugiru. English
Description: First Yen On edition. I New York : Yen On, 2019–
Identifiers: LCCN 2019013049 I ISBN 9781975356880 (v. 1 ; pbk.)
Subjects: GSAFD: Fantasy fiction.
Classification: LCC PL876.U34 K5613 2019 I DDC 895.63/6—dc23
LC record available at https://lccn.loc.gov/2019013049

ISBNs: 978-1-9753-5688-0 (paperback)
978-1-9753-5689-7 (ebook)

10 9 8 7 6 5 4 3 2 1

LSC-C

Printed in the United States of America

CONTENTS

The Hero Is Overpowered but Overly Cautious

PROLOGUE
A Goddess's Despair

"I hereby announce that Ristarte will be the goddess in charge of saving the S-ranked world Gaeabrande!"

Roaring applause echoes throughout the sanctuary of this unified spirit world, a separate dimension from the world in which humans reside. From every direction, I'm showered with the thunderous applause of virile men and gorgeous women.

"What a rewarding mission! You can do it, Rista!"

"Wow, Rista! You'll be a full-fledged goddess once this is over!"

Cheered on by my superiors, I force a smile onto my face.

An S-ranked world…? You've got to be kidding me…

I, Ristarte, was born into this unified spirit world as a goddess around one hundred years ago. Since then, I have summoned Heroes five times from the human realm in order to save worlds in peril. And, well, five times is quite a bit less compared to the other seasoned gods and goddesses. On average, one would usually perform several dozen summons in this time frame while some even manage to perform a few hundred to save various human worlds. Incidentally, S-ranked worlds are frightening lands that make even the most experienced gods wince. Why? Because the evil beings that are trying to dominate these worlds are said to have powers that rival the gods'.

After returning to the room I was assigned in the sanctuary, I take out my list of candidates, consisting solely of relatively young Japanese people from the planet Earth. Ever since my third summons, I've been making it a point to summon only young Heroes from Japan. As a side note, the first Hero I summoned was from Mars, and the second Hero was an aborigine from a remote village in South Africa. It took an entire month to get them up to speed.

In Japan, however, there exists fiction about being transported to parallel universes or being reborn in other worlds. These tales are apparently quite popular, which makes explaining things easy. And, well, although the fad is waning, it's still popular in Japan and is taking the market by storm and—Ack. What in the world am I even rambling on about? I must be exhausted.

It shouldn't come as a surprise, though. I've been looking through piles of lists of candidates in my room for a while now, after all. My face has become oily, I have bags under my eyes, and to crown it all, I can't stop nervously tapping my foot. After spending all that time brushing my gorgeous long blond hair, it's already a mess. Still, even if it means sacrificing my beauty as a goddess, I continue gazing at two candidates' abstracts I managed to select from the mountain of lists stacked on my desk.

Let's take a look at the first candidate.

ATSUSHI SASAKI

LV: 1

HP: 101   MP: 0

ATK: 55   DEF: 37   SPD: 28   MAG: 0   GRW: 6

Resistance: None

Special Abilities: None

Personality: Normal

...He appears to be a Warrior. While he doesn't have any magic, his attack power is high. Plus, unlike most of the other candidates, his initial HP of 101 is in the triple digits. All right, let's take a look at the second candidate.

YUUKO SUZUKI

LV: 1

HP: 65   **MP: 47**

ATK: 18   **DEF: 29**   **SPD: 20**   **MAG: 72**   **GRW: 7**

Resistance: Water

Special Abilities: Fire Magic (LV: 1)

Personality: Normal

...This one's your basic Mage-type Hero. Being able to use fire magic right from the start and being resistant to water magic are both good traits.

So is it going to be Sasaki or Suzuki? Suzuki or Sasaki? I'd prefer to take them both with me, but I can summon only one Hero per world. Suzuki, Sasaki, Sasaki, Suzuki, Suzuki, Sasaki—even their names sound similar. I'm starting to not care which one I choose...

I place the two résumés I selected back onto the desk before letting out a deep sigh.

"I can't wait to get more experience and become a high-ranking goddess!"

I know I've been saying that almost every day to my superiors, but this isn't at all what I had in mind. If this were a C-ranked or D-ranked world like usual, then neither Sasaki nor Suzuki would be a problem. But this is Gaeabrande, an S-ranked world. I have to be extra careful with who I choose. The more I think about it, the more I feel that maybe neither of them would be the right choice.

I—I guess I'll just have to look through all the lists again. Besides, I might have accidentally overlooked someone...

However, I suddenly start feeling dizzy before the mountain of documents on my desk and fall flat into my chair...causing the stack of papers to collapse onto my head.

"Gyaaahhhhhh!"

After letting out a scream unfit for a goddess, I find myself buried in paper. I bitterly swat the documents away from me, but one résumé is stuck to my forehead, and I can't get it off.

"Stupid...paper...! Ugh!"

Annoyed, I manage to peel it off and give it a look.

...But I can hardly believe my eyes.

SEIYA RYUUGUUIN

LV: 1

HP: 385   **MP: 197**

ATK: 124   **DEF: 111**   **SPD: 105**   **MAG: 86**   **GRW: 188**

Resistance: Fire, Ice, Wind, Water, Lightning, Earth

Special Abilities: Fire Magic (LV: 5), EXP Boost (LV: 2)

Personality: Overly Cautious

"...Huh?"

H-h-hold up. Wait. What's going on here? I mean, his stats are incredible for someone who's only level 1.

Am I hallucinating due to fatigue? Is the stress making me delusional?

I rub my eyes and stare at the sheet of paper so hard, I could burn a hole through it, but the numbers don't change.

I-I've never seen a human with stats like this before! He's perfect! Undoubtedly a man of extraordinary talent! He's one in a million—no, one in a billion!

Tightly grasping the résumé, I dash out of the room and head over to see the Great Goddess Ishtar...

My heart racing, I proceed to the Summoning Chamber after finishing the application. When I was first told that I was going to be in charge of managing an S-ranked world, I cursed my ill fate… I never even dreamed I would encounter a Hero with such amazing stats! He'll be able to save Gaeabrande in no time, and I'll be one step closer to becoming a Great Goddess! I mean, seriously, am I lucky or what?!

Seiya Ryuuguuin—what an imposing name.

I skip down the marble passage, utterly captivated by his impressive stats…which is how I overlooked a certain detail. Or more precisely, I saw it, but it simply didn't seem that important at the time.

Personality: Overly Cautious

It's not long after the summoning that I regret my actions.

CHAPTER 1
I Refuse

When I open the hinged double doors, I find myself in a room that's completely white as far as the eye can see. The Summoning Chamber is what you would call a pocket dimension and boasts a vast radius of a few kilometers, despite being contained within the sanctuary.

I take a few dozen steps into the room, then stop short to retrieve a golden stick of chalk from the bust of my dress. Thereupon, I draw a magic circle on the ground and begin reading the Hero's name aloud. Seeing that this is my sixth time, I'm getting pretty good at this if I do say so myself. Before long, the magic circle illuminates, and a man is summoned from the earthly realm.

Oh... Oh no...! H-he's...! He's so dreamy!

He's over 180 centimeters tall with youthful-looking black locks hanging over his masculine face. He's wearing a T-shirt and jeans, common attire for the average person in his world, but there doesn't seem to be anything average about him. Even the aura radiating from his body is as awe-inspiring as the gods of the spirit world.

Oh, how I wish just once I could fall deeply in love with a man like this and— Ack! Wh-what's wrong with me?! Love between goddesses and humans is prohibited!

I mentally shake my head. At any rate, this human is so attractive that I almost lost all sense of discipline as a goddess.

But I notice something. The man is staring at me in silence and understandably so. After all, who wouldn't be startled after suddenly being whisked away from the life they once knew and summoned to a completely white room? I speak to the man with an air of authority in my voice.

"It is a pleasure to finally meet you. I am Ristarte, a goddess of this unified spirit world. I have summoned you to this dimension for a certain mission. Seiya Ryuuguuin, you shall become the Hero who saves the parallel world Gaeabrande from the evil clutches of the Demon Lord."

I confidently chuckle.

As expected, Seiya continues silently staring at me. He seems more enchanted by me than surprised. It's understandable, though. I don't mean to brag, but I am a goddess. And to put it bluntly, I'm very attractive: gorgeous, glossy blond hair; a pure-white dress with ample breasts, a bit of cleavage showing; and a slim waist accompanied by slender legs. My beauty must have left him speechless. I doubt this Seiya person has ever seen such a perfect woman in his life. I inwardly chuckle to myself...until Seiya finally speaks in a lowered tone.

"To think you'd drop a bomb like this on a complete stranger... You're a weird one, aren't you?"

"'Weird'?! Are you talking about me?!"

Uh-oh... The real me slipped out for a moment there. Th-this isn't good! Dignity! I must maintain my dignity as a goddess!

After clearing my throat, I try to speak calmly to him.

"I am not weird. Allow me to repeat myself. I am a goddess—a goddess of the heavens who summoned you, Hero."

"A goddess, huh? If you're really a goddess, then why don't you just save that parallel world yourself?"

"Th-there are rules. The gods created countless worlds to flourish at the hands of humans. That's why only humans themselves can save human worlds."

Seiya heaves a deep sigh.

"Do I even have a choice?"

"No."

Upon hearing this, Seiya casts a disgusted glare at me.

"You're asking too much of me."

The *he's wonderful!* feeling I had earlier steadily withers away with that brazen attitude of his.

Wh-what a peculiar man. Most people are ecstatic when I tell them they were chosen to be a Hero… O-oh, well. He's probably just confused after being summoned so suddenly. Good thing I have the perfect remedy for situations like this! I'll just sidle up to Seiya like so, aaand…

"Hey, Seiya! I want you to yell 'status,' okay?"

Heh-heh-heh! This! This is it! This is perfect! Japanese people love stuff like this!

"Why?"

"Huh? Wait. You don't know? Were you not that into video games? Ah, it doesn't matter. Whenever you yell 'status,' you'll be able to see your capabilities expressed in numerical form! Anyway, just give it a go! Seeing is believing!"

However, after a brief moment of silence…

"…Properties."

"'Properties'?!"

I'm pretty sure I told him to say "status," so why did he say that?! What is that even supposed to mean?!

Seiya appraises the information on the screen that appears before him and nods.

"I see. There actually is information here that only I would know. I guess that makes your bullshit story a little more credible."

…Does he not realize how disrespectful he's being to a goddess?!

"A-anyway, forget about 'properties.' Just say 'status,' okay? Come on. Please? I'm begging you!"

Seiya reluctantly mutters "status" in response to my heartfelt appeal. Thereupon, a three-dimensional screen pops up just like before. I look over his shoulder to read his status with him.

"Well? What do you think? I don't know if you can tell, but your stats are amazing! They're way higher than your average Hero's! Listen, your talent is one in a billion! You, Seiya Ryuuguuin, are the only one who can defeat the powerful Demon Lord of Gaeabrande!"

I say everything I can to fire him up, but he doesn't seem all that happy. In fact, he looks pensive, as if his mind was elsewhere.

"By the way, what happens if I die in that world?"

"W-well, that's a pessimistic way to look at it…but there's no need to worry! You'll simply return to the world from whence you came! However, you will never be able to return to this world after that…"

Seiya gives a dismissive snort as if to suggest that anything I say or do is of no concern to him. I've had a sneaking suspicion ever since we started talking: He's the kind of person who has to see something to believe it. That's it!

"Seiya! I'll explain later! But for now, let's go to Gaeabrande!"

I immediately cast a spell, opening a gate before us to Gaeabrande. With the gate open, I call out to him.

"Seiya Ryuuguuin! Join me! The fate of Gaeabrande is in your hands!"

"I refuse."

"Now then, I bet you're so excited to see what kind of world Gaeabrande is, right? …Wait, huh? W-wait! Wait, wait, wait! What did you just say?"

"I said I refuse. Do you seriously think I would go to such a dangerous world on a whim without even preparing?"

"B-but your stats are considerably higher than most people's. Besides, I'll take the form of a human while in Gaeabrande, and I'll always be with you to help. So don't worry abo—"

"Didn't you say the human world had to be saved by humans? I doubt you'd be very useful."

"H-how rude! I'm a goddess, you know! I won't die, and I can even heal you with magic when you get hurt!"

"See, what did I tell you? You'd have a back-seat role, making you essentially useless when it comes to saving the world."

Ugh! H-how dare he talk to a goddess like that! I—I would love to beat his face in right about now!

However, Seiya delivers another cold, piercing glare.

"If I don't have a choice in the matter, at least let me prepare."

"P-prepare? By doing what exactly…?"

CHAPTER 2
Perfectly Prepared

"He is beyond weird!"

"...So what ended up happening?"

I wound up complaining to Ariadoa in her room. Aria, a redheaded goddess and my senior, is taller than me and has a certain mature, sensual charm to her, despite being in the prime of her youth. She's a seasoned goddess, having summoned Heroes to over three hundred worlds.

"He said he had to prepare, but then he just started working out in the Summoning Chamber! Can you believe it? If I were him, I'd want to get out of that blinding white room as soon as possible. I mean, wouldn't most people be excited to see another world? It makes no sense!"

Aria giggles.

"Rista, you're going to be saving an S-ranked world. It's probably a good thing your Hero is being this cautious."

"Yeah, but he's, like, wasting his time, you know? I mean, he'd level up a lot quicker if he'd just go to Gaeabrande and start fighting monsters."

"What's the rush? Time moves slower in the spirit world, and that includes the Summoning Chamber. You might as well let him stay here until he's mentally prepared."

"...*Sigh*. I just wanted to go on a normal adventure."

Aria calmly sips her tea. Being more mature and experienced than I am, she then smiles and says:

"Listen, Rista. You just need to support him. If he's training in the Summoning Chamber right now, then you need to be there for him."

"...How?"

"Well, did you remember to put a toilet, shower, and bed in that dreary room? He's going to get hungry, too, you know?"

"Ah...! Now that you mention it...!"

As I begin to rush out of the room, Aria stops me one last time.

"One more thing, Rista. People like him probably don't like being told what to do, so try opening up to him and talking to him like you would to a friend."

That's Aria for you—a true pro. After a quick thank-you, I close the door and immediately rush down the marble corridor.

"Seiya! I'm so sorry for leaving you alone for so long. I..."

When I open the large door to the Summoning Chamber, I find Seiya shirtless and doing sit-ups. Beads of sweat cling to his body. It's so sexy that I can't look away. That's when he begins glaring at me.

"Hey. Could you at least knock before you come barging in next time?"

"S-sorry."

...Hang on! This is the Summoning Chamber, not your own private gym!

I fight the urge to give him a piece of my mind but instead reveal the rice balls I brought.

"I—I, uh... I thought you might be hungry, so I made these for you."

"...What are they?"

I flash a cheery smile.

"You're Japanese, right? I actually know a lot about Japan! Look, rice balls! This one's pickled plum, and this one's salmon. Also—"

Before I even finish my sentence, Seiya stares at the rice balls I made and snorts in disgust.

"Suspicious food made by a suspicious person, huh?"

"...?! How rude!"

"You eat one first."

"What?!"

"They could be poisoned."

...I took Aria's advice and tried to be nice, so I made him some rice balls. And yet, here I am, already wanting to strangle him.

"They're not poisoned! How stupid can you be?! Why would I even try to poison you?!"

Annoyed, I bite into the salmon rice ball.

"See?! No poison! Happy now?! Ugh! Unbelievable! Do you know how hard I worked to make these for you?!"

"Hmm... There doesn't seem to be any fast-acting poison in them."

"Because there isn't any poison in them at all, dammit!"

I scream at Seiya, using crass language unbecoming of a goddess.

"And just so you know, working out and doing push-ups and sit-ups in this room isn't going to raise your abilities that much!"

After screaming at the top of my lungs, I use my divine powers to instantly create a portable toilet, a portable shower, and a cot. Then I sternly shove a buzzer in Seiya's hand.

"Buzz me if you need me! You will be eating three meals a day, and they will be slid under the door! I will, under no circumstances, be coming here again until you press that buzzer!"

"Good."

After slamming the door on my way out, I return to my room, stamping my feet the entire way.

What is wrong with him?! Whatever. I'll just leave him alone for now. It's not like someone can live in that empty room forever! I give him two, three days tops before he rings the buzzer!

...But Seiya never rang the buzzer. After four days went by, I was starting to doubt he was even alive, but he seemed to be eating the rice balls left for him. Despite saying that I wouldn't be visiting him no matter what, I couldn't help but pay frequent visits to the Summoning Chamber and place an ear to the door to make sure he was all right.

...Then, after a week, Seiya finally rings the buzzer. I rush over to the chamber and open the door, only to be welcomed by the pleasant scent of soap wafting from his body. He must have just gotten out of the shower.

"S-so? How did your training go?"

Seiya simply mutters "status" and opens a three-dimensional window. I faintly gasp the moment I see it.

SEIYA RYUUGUUIN

LV: 15

HP: 2,485   MP: 1,114

ATK: 533   DEF: 507   SPD: 623   MAG: 499   GRW: 341

Resistance: Fire, Ice, Wind, Water, Lightning, Earth, Paralysis, Sleep

Special Abilities: Fire Magic (LV: 9), EXP Boost (LV: 3), Scan (LV: 5)

Skills: Atomic Split Slash, Hellfire

Personality: Overly Cautious

"H-he gained this many levels just from training in his room?!"

I'm sure his EXP Boost is helping, but never in my wildest dreams did I expect growth like this. With stats like these, he would honestly have a chance against the Demon Lord in the D-rank world I just saved. As I stand there in astonishment, Seiya casually states:

"Ideally, I would like to raise myself to the max level, but…"

"Do you plan on living in this room for the rest of your life?! Yes, time is slower while you're in this dimension, but even then, you'd die before you reached the max level! You've leveled up enough already! Let's get a move on! Gaeabrande is waiting for us!"

Seiya quietly nods after my rant.

"Yeah, you're probably right…"

While idly staring into the distance of this completely white Summoning Chamber, he says:

"I'm perfectly prepared."

*   *   *

Wh-what the…?! Now he's trying to act cool?! Give me a break!

"Ugh. Whatever. Let's just go."

I cast a spell, once again summoning the gate to the new world. Then I snatch Seiya's hand and head toward it.

And that's how we end up departing for Gaeabrande a week late.

CHAPTER 3
To the Town of Edona

We walk through the gate and find ourselves on a prairie. However, I can also see a peaceful town only a few dozen meters ahead. Our journey begins at the ideal location thanks to Great Goddess Ishtar fine-tuning the gate for us. Seiya, however, continues to stare as it fades into nothingness. So I pat him on the back to get him moving.

"Come on! Let's head to that town over there and buy some new equipment!"

Seiya looks like he wants to say something, but I take him by the hand and lead him to the nearby town.

The standing wooden signboard says WELCOME TO EDONA! We pass under the sign, then continue down the unpaved path until we stroll by some people wearing farm clothes. The pastoral atmosphere makes Edona seem to be more of a village than a town.

"Oh, a couple travelers, eh? Welcome, welcome."

Without hesitation, I bow to the farmer with a smile, but Seiya seems suspicious. After the farmers move on, he whispers to me:

"Hey, was that a monster?"

"Th-that was just a villager. Could you seriously not tell...?"

"I thought he might have been a monster that transformed into a villager."

"You're overthinking things…"

After going a bit farther, we are approached by a young girl wearing her hair in two braids. The moment the five- or six-year-old child sees me, she cheerfully smiles from ear to ear.

"Wow! You're so pretty! Like a goddess!"

"Tee-hee. Innocent children sure know perfection when they see it, don't they?"

Elated, I pat the girl on the head. She then looks up at Seiya.

"Hey, mister! Your clothes are strange, but you're cool, too!"

The little girl walks away from me and tightly latches onto his jeans. There is something about Seiya's rare troubled face that pleases me a little.

"Well, well. If there's a little kid around, I guess even *you* can be nice."

Seiya simply replies with a brief "hmph" as the little girl continues looking up at him.

"Hey, mister, what's your name?"

"…"

"Heeey, what's your name?"

"…Seiya."

"Oh, neat! I'm Nina! Nice to meet you!"

I wish I had more time to watch their exchange, but we don't have any to waste.

"Hey, Nina, could you tell us where the weapon shop is?"

"Um… It's right up ahead!"

"I see! Thanks a bunch!"

After waving good-bye to Nina, we follow her directions and walk straight ahead. Before long, we find ourselves on a street packed with shops. Seiya and I stop before a sign with a sword painted on it. I hand him a small pouch.

"Here, this is my gift to you. With this much money, you should be able to buy the best equipment this town has to offer."

This is actually this world's currency, which I asked Great Goddess Ishtar to prepare for us. After walking around the shop, Seiya takes all the gold coins out of the pouch and hands them to the chubby middle-aged store owner.

"I'll take three suits of steel armor."

"Coming right up!"

As the shop owner goes to get three suits of armor...

"Whoooa! Hang on a sec!"

I desperately convince the shop owner to stay put before scolding Seiya.

"You do *not* need that much armor!"

"Yes I do. One to wear, a spare, and another spare in case I lose the spare."

This isn't simply being overcautious anymore. It's definitely weird. I don't care what world he's from. Who in their right mind would spend all their gold coins on three suits of the same armor?!

"Just stand over there! I'm choosing what we're buying!"

"Well, aren't you controlling."

I purchase a steel sword and one (I repeat, *one*) suit of armor. I force Seiya to equip the items on the spot, and he ends up looking rather sharp, partly thanks to his tall, muscular physique. Appearance-wise, he actually looks like a half-decent warrior.

After leaving the weapon shop, Seiya goes off on his own to the item shop next door. Then, after listening to the shopkeeper's explanation of the items...

"I'll take ten smoke bombs and twenty herbs. Twenty antidotes as well, thanks."

Seiya scoops up all the items he can get with the leftover money. I don't feel the need to stop him, since these are relatively cheap compared to weapons and armor. However, I still can't help but ask him something after we leave the shop.

"Hey, uh... Do you really need to take this many precautions?"

"I have no idea what kinds of vicious monsters lurk in the shadows. Of course I'm going to take precautions."

"Don't worry so much. I may not look it, but I'm an experienced navigator, you know. I arranged our start near a town that would be suitable for you. All the monsters around here are weak."

"I wonder about that."

Just then...

"Yeah, it'll be fine! I wouldn't even worry about that!"

I suddenly hear a familiar voice coming from below. Lowering my gaze, I see Nina from earlier cheerfully smiling at me.

"Even I can walk to the nearby town without worrying about monsters! There are only slimes around here!"

She must have been listening to our conversation. I pat Nina on the head while sending Seiya a reproachful gaze.

"See? Even a little girl isn't worried about the monsters here. Feel better now?"

"Are you scared to leave town, mister? You look really strong, though…"

"This mister right here is a big, fat scaredy-cat."

I thought Nina and I could team up and verbally abuse him together, but her innocence exceeds my imagination. She takes a pressed flower pouch made of cloth out of her pocket, then retrieves something from it and hands it to Seiya.

"Here, it's for good luck!"

Seiya takes a hard look at the pressed flower in his hand.

"You didn't just give me a cursed item, did you?"

"Huh?"

I clap a hand over Seiya's mouth.

"D-don't worry about him! He's a little sick in the head! Just a bit of mental illness! That's all!"

That's when a man comes screaming at Nina from behind.

"Nina! What are you doing?!"

"Ah! Papa! Did you finish shopping already?"

The gentle-looking father bows to us.

"I-I'm so sorry. I hope my daughter didn't say or do anything rude."

"She was a perfect little angel. Right?"

As I turn my gaze to Seiya, he averts his own and briskly mutters…

"Yeah, she's fine."

Huh, maybe he's not such a bad guy after all…is something I might say if I were drunk.

CHAPTER 4
First Monster

We leave town after getting some rather high-quality equipment and wander over to a field in search of monsters for Seiya to fight. He wasn't on board with the idea at first, but perhaps his pride wouldn't allow him to refuse after hearing that even Nina travels outside of town alone from time to time. Now he's following me without so much as a single complaint. Before long, I find exactly what I'm looking for. A sky-blue bouncy ball of goo jiggles in the shadows of the tall grass before us.

"Seiya, look! It's a monster!"

"Huh, what a bizarre creature. The result of gene manipulation, perhaps?"

"It's a magical creature! A slime! Haven't you seen them in video games before?"

I am astonished to see him shake his head. H-he doesn't know what a slime is? I thought everyone in Japan knew...

"Seiya, slimes will jump at you and attack the moment they see you. Their mucus can melt your skin, but it won't cause too much damage if you wipe it off right away. They're so weak that the average adult could defeat one with a wooden club. But—what the...?"

My eyes go wide as saucers. Seiya draws his steel sword from the sheath, then quietly exhales. The blade begins glowing as if reacting to his breathing. The air around us vibrates.

"Eat this…! Atomic Split Slash!"

In the very next moment, Seiya aims his sword at the slime and slashes. The shock wave sounds like an explosion, splitting the ground where the slime once sat!

"Eeeeeeek!!"

As the gale makes a mess of my hair, I scream out to Seiya.

"Wh-what is wrong with you?! It's just a slime! You're overdoing it!"

But he points his left hand at the ruined patch of earth that's clearly empty.

"No…! It could still be alive!"

After that, Seiya's left hand is engulfed in roaring flames.

"Hellfire!"

At once, magical flames shoot from his hand, scorching the empty space. And in the blink of an eye, the entire grassy field is reduced to ashes.

"It's already dead, dammit! You're fighting nothing! Nothiiiiiing!"

But my screams have no effect.

"No… It's still too risky to let my guard down…"

Seiya takes a stance with his sword once again.

What the…?! But he only has two skills! Wh-what does he plan on doing next?!

As if in response to my mental anguish, he takes another deep breath and his sword brims with such intense power that the air itself trembles.

"Atomic Split Slash!"

"You're using Atomic Split Slash *again*?!"

The echo of the blast roars throughout the field. There's an explosion, a heavy rumble, and the ground splits open yet again. My hair is violently buffeted by another strong gust of wind.

…After a while, it starts to look like I'm standing in a crater left by a comet strike. And at long last, after the Hero casually sheathes his sword, I scream:

"Why the hell are you attacking a single slime with everything you've got?! You obliterated it the second you used your Atomic-whatever attack the first time!"

"Carelessness is the greatest enemy."

"There's a limit to everything, you know! Besides, don't you have the ability Scan?! Did you not check its stats?!"

"I did just to make sure. Its attack and defense were in the single digits."

"Then why did you unload on it like that?!"

"It's not enough to rely only on what you can see in front of you. Even though we can't see the slime anymore, that doesn't mean it's dead."

"...?! Have more faith in your abilities!!"

I expel a deep sigh while fixing my hair.

"Anyway, you must be feeling a bit more confident now, right? You're extremely strong, so let's start making our way to the next town. According to the information I got from the Great Goddess, we should be finding your first ally there..."

Right as I place a hand on Seiya's shoulder, I sense an evil presence that makes the hairs on the back of my neck stand up.

"Wh-what?"

I turn around to find a woman slowly walking our way. Her hair is as black as crow feathers, and she dresses in revealing bikini-like attire of the same color. With one hand, she carries a claymore that's as tall as she is, making the act look effortless. She appears to be a warrior, but her sinister aura is proof that she is no human. The woman flashes Seiya an alluring smile.

"That was some impreeessive swordsmanship. You're the one, aaaren't you? Nooo, I'm certain it's you."

"Wh-who are you?" I ask in Seiya's place, causing the woman's lips to curl into a devilish grin.

"It's a pleeeasure to welcome you to our dimension, Oh Hero chosen by the goddess. I am Chaos Machina, one of the four generals of the Demon Lord's army."

The shocking revelation sends a chill down my spine.

Th-this can't be happening! What's one of the Demon Lord's generals doing so close to the starting town?! That's impossible! Ishtar sent us to a safe haven to start our journey, and yet...!

But the sinister, beast-like aura oozing from her every pore makes me painfully aware that she's telling the truth. Chaos Machina suppresses a laugh as if she can sense my restlessness.

"Surpriiised? The Demon Lord saw signs that the Hero was going to be summoned before you even arrived. He apparently wasn't able to predict exactly where you would appear, though. But, but, buuut if you're going to summon a Hero, you're going to want him to start off in a place where the monsters are weak, riiight? That's why I decided to randomly investigate the villages and cities like that until I found traces of an unfamiliar person…aaand here I am!"

She looks like she's enjoying herself, but I still break out into a cold sweat.

W-well…that's the S-ranked world Gaeabrande for you! Anything I considered common sense in the lower-ranked worlds won't apply here!

"The Demon Lord was rather wary of you, but it's possible that he was just overreacting, riiight? But, but, buuut after actually meeting you, I can tell. You have the potential to become increeedibly powerful. Nope, nope, nope, nope. We can't have that! You need to be dealt with immeeediately."

Chaos Machina playfully pokes out her tongue, then brandishes her massive sword.

Th-this is bad! She's serious about this!

I brace myself before using Scan to check her stats and…well……we're doomed.

CHAOS MACHINA

LV: 66

HP: 3,877   MP: 108

ATK: 887   DEF: 845   SPD: 951   MAG: 444   GRW: 653

Resistance: Wind, Water

Special Abilities: Magic Sword (LV: 15)

Skills: Demonic Curse

Personality: Cruel

Wh-wh-what?! These are not the stats of an enemy you run into at the beginning of the journey!

"S-Seiya…!"

Despite being a goddess, I freak out over the appearance of a horrifying opponent and shamelessly turn around to Seiya for help.

…But suddenly, he's nowhere to be found.

"Are you kidding me?!"

I let out a hysterical cry, for I find the Hero…running off into the distance like a frightened rabbit.

"H-hey! H-how dare you leave a goddess behind and run off! Get back here!"

As I'm chasing after him, I can hear Chaos Machina laughing in the background.

"Oh my, my, my, myyy! What kind of Hero leaves his goddess behind and runs awaaay? You made the right decision, though! Most people wouldn't be able to make such a quick judgment call and immediately act on it! This Hero is so very, very, very iiinteresting!"

There are no signs of her coming after us. I call out to Seiya while running with everything I've got.

"P-please! Just wait a moment!"

That's when Seiya slows his pace and looks back…before immediately throwing something at me.

Boom!

"Eek!"

Something explodes by my feet, engulfing the entire area in a thick fog.

"What is your problem?!"

As I seethe with rage, I hear the *whoosh* of air being displaced by a massive blade. I thought she wasn't following us anymore, but Chaos Machina is somehow already behind me. She swings her colossal sword right at my neck.

"Ha-ha-ha! A smoke screen, huuuh? Once again, your judgment is impeeeccable!"

Chaos Machina laughs again. As I grope around in the thick cloud of smoke, I feel a hand grab me by the arm. Before I even realize it, I'm being pulled away by Seiya. He speaks to me in his usual calm voice, completely unfazed by our current dilemma.

"Hey. We're retreating. Hurry and open the gate to the unified spirit world or whatever."

"G-good idea! Okay!"

Running as quickly as I can, I cast the spell, creating the gate a few dozen meters ahead. We run until there are only a few centimeters left, but a demon's voice echoes from behind...

"You're not getting awaaaaaay!!"

When I glance back, the demon general makes a powerful leap from the smoke and swings her sword. I let out a faint scream and look to Seiya for help...but he's already heading toward Chaos Machina with his left hand in the air, engulfed in a crimson blaze. Then the wavelike flames of Hellfire spread as if overflowing from his hand. Rather than an all-out attack, Seiya seems to be using the flames as a distraction to slow her down. Engulfed by the inferno, Chaos Machina clicks her tongue, a dark expression on her face. And just like that, we seize the opportunity to open the gate and escape.

CHAPTER 5
The Worst Hero

"Th-that was a close one, huh?"

After tumbling out of the gate, I immediately close it. I was in a hurry, so I didn't have time to choose a destination, which is why I'm now crouching in the snow-white Summoning Chamber trying to catch my breath. Seiya, on the other hand, has his breathing under control.

"It's pretty lucky that we ended up here. I'd better start training at once."

Then he shoves my back while I continue panting.

"E-excuse me?"

"You'll be a distraction. Get out."

"Y-you're going to do more weight training?"

"Yep. I won't be able to defeat her if I don't. And from the looks of it, she's a lot stronger than that slime."

"Y-yeah, I mean…she *is* one of the four generals of the Demon Lord's army…"

"I am not leaving this room until I achieve the desired results. I'll buzz you when I'm ready. Don't bother me before then."

Seeing his eyes brimming with determination leaves me speechless. And so Seiya kicks me out and locks himself in the Summoning Chamber once again.

…Two nights have passed. As I slide Seiya's breakfast under the door, I suddenly get a bad feeling. Call it a goddess's intuition. After borrowing Aria's crystal ball, capable of displaying an unobstructed view of the human world, and bringing it back to my room, I place it in front of me and cast a spell.

"Oh, all-knowing crystal, if there is imminent danger in the world, let it be revealed…"

At once, an image of the town of Edona appears within the crystal ball—centering around the heart of the city's businesses…

…when suddenly…

"Heeey, can you see me?"

"Ahhh!"

Chaos Machina's ominous face pops up on the crystal ball, almost giving me a heart attack. Wearing an alluring smirk, she yells:

"Someone's sneaking a peek, aren't they? Could it be the goddess and her Hero? Just so you know, if you two don't show up soon, I'm going to destroy this town, okaaay?"

Then, as if Chaos Machina knows exactly where I'm watching from, she grabs an innocent man by the head with one hand and forcibly faces him in my direction as he weeps in terror.

"For every ten minutes you don't show up, I'm going to cut off a villager's head."

Without a moment of hesitation, the colossal blade glides through the air and cleanly separates the crying man's head from his shoulders. Fresh blood sprays in every direction, and I have to look away.

"The fountains of red that gush from humans are so very, very, very beauuutiful."

Even through the crystal ball, I can hear the ecstasy in Chaos Machina's voice.

WHAM!

I fling open the door to the Summoning Chamber, catching Seiya in the middle of training. He shoots me a piercing glare.

"I told you not to come here until I rang the buzzer."

"It's an emergency! We have to go back to Edona! Now!"

"Why?"

"Because Chaos Machina is executing villagers, and she won't stop until we show ourselves! Now hurry up and get ready!"

I plead with Seiya, but he doesn't stop training.

"No. I haven't fully prepared yet."

"But…! Chaos Machina is killing villagers as we speak!"

"Relax. Weren't you the one who said that time moves more slowly here?"

"That doesn't mean it stops completely!"

"Then could you tell me the exact difference in time between this space and that one?"

"…Time moves almost one hundred times slower here. Ten minutes there is sixteen hours here."

"Then there isn't a problem. We still have plenty of time before the next guy gets killed."

…Well, yes, but wouldn't most Heroes want to rush over to save the villagers as quickly as possible?! What is with him?!

I impatiently return to my room but start feeling uneasy and gaze into the crystal ball again.

…How many hours have gone by?

Before long, Chaos Machina makes her move and grabs another hostage by the neck.

"Looks like this guy's up neeext."

I know that man, but I'm not entirely sure how I know him until I hear a certain voice through the crystal ball.

"PAPA!! NOOO!! LET HIM GOOOOO!!"

A small girl who wears her hair in two braids is howling and crying. The moment I see her, I pick up the crystal ball and make a dash for the Summoning Chamber. When I open the door, Seiya glares at me as if fed up.

"How many times do I have to tell you to stay out?"

"Who cares about that?! Look at this! You know who that is, right? It's Nina! Her dad's about to be killed!"

But Seiya doesn't even flinch. Instead, he starts doing one-handed push-ups.

"H-hey! Are you even listening?"

"I haven't fully prepared yet."

At that moment, I feel like I've caught a glimpse of Seiya's mind while he trains. I decide to have a heart-to-heart with him.

"Seiya, I know it's scary. But with your stats, you really do have a fighting chance against her, and I'll make sure to back you up as much as I can. My healing magic isn't too shabby if I do say so myself. So…? What do you say?"

But his stare practically screams, *Are you stupid?*

"What are you talking about? I'm not scared."

"Says the guy who ran away from her."

"That was a tactical retreat."

His stubbornness causes me to explode with rage.

"We're leaving! Now! Okay?! Even if you happen to die, you'll just be sent back to the world you came from! But those villagers won't! Once they're dead, there's no bringing them back!"

Even after all that, Seiya still refuses to listen to me. The only sounds that can be heard are Nina's heart-wrenching cries as a heavy silence falls over the Summoning Chamber.

"Papaaa! No! Please don't…! Please don't kill him!"

Chaos Machina gives Nina a wicked grin.

"Don't wooorry, little one. You won't be lonely. You won't be lonely at all! Because after I cut your papa's head off, you're next, okaaay?"

I hold the crystal ball right in Seiya's face.

"Seiya! Do you feel nothing?! This little girl gave you a flower! She was worried about you, so she gave you her good luck charm!"

He takes the pressed flower out of his pocket and glances at it.

"Hmm… It looks like this flower really is a cursed item. I probably would've never run into that woman if I didn't have it."

I'm in shock.

"I failed… I'm a failure…!"

Seiya reacts to the words dribbling out of my mouth.

"Why?"

"Because I summoned you! You might have good stats, but you're a terrible Hero! The worst!"

Tears well up in my eyes. It's so frustrating that I can't even contain myself. As I start walking out the door, Seiya stops me.

"What are you going to do? Is there someone other than me who can defeat Chaos Machina?"

"I'll find someone else! I'm going to go get a Hero to replace you!"

"You said that my talents were one in a billion when you first saw my status, so I highly doubt you'll be able to find a replacement that easily."

"I'll find someone else even if it kills me! There are plenty of Heroes who could replace a coward like you!"

"I'm not a coward."

"Coward! Just admit you're afraid to die! That's why you're being so careful and preparing so much! Am I wrong?!"

"I'm not afraid to die. I just can't afford to, because if I do, that village will be destroyed. And before long, that entire world will be destroyed along with it."

…I can't believe what I'm hearing.

H-he's actually thinking with the world's interest in m— Wait! No, that can't be! I can't be taken in by his words! He's just making excuses and trying to sound cool to hide the fact that he's a coward!

I shoot him a distant glare, but he's already on the move. He's removing his training gear and equipping the steel armor.

"Wh-what are you doing?"

"What does it look like?"

"W-wait… Don't tell me you're…!"

I use Scan and peek at his status.

SEIYA RYUUGUUIN

LV: 21

HP: 4,412   MP: 2,367

ATK: 932   DEF: 990   SPD: 993   MAG: 666   GRW: 475

Resistance: Fire, Ice, Wind, Water, Lightning, Earth, Paralysis, Sleep, Curse, Instant Death

Special Abilities: Fire Magic (LV: 18), EXP Boost (LV: 6), Scan (LV: 8)

Skills: Atomic Split Slash, Hellfire

Personality: Overly Cautious

H-how did he get this strong in such a short period of time?! His stats even surpass the Demon General Chaos Machina...!

A man whose talents are one in a billion—Seiya Ryuuguuin, dressed in steel armor, sends me a penetrating gaze.

"I'm perfectly prepared."

CHAPTER 6
Ace in the Hole

"All right, I'm opening us a gate to the center of the village!"

As I'm about to cast the spell, Seiya smacks me on the back of the head.

"Ouch! What now?!"

"Are you stupid? How does that sound like a good idea to you? Make the gate connect to somewhere farther away."

"B-but if we don't hurry and save them…"

"I'm telling you this *to* save them. Her personality is cruel, correct? She would most likely kill that man the moment she sees me. She wouldn't need a hostage anymore, after all."

H-huh, that actually makes sense. But…

"Sure, but could you not hit me in the head next time?!"

He appears a bit remorseful when I get mad at him, which is unusual.

"All right, I'll make sure to be careful from now on."

Wh-what the…? He's owning up to it?

"G-good…"

Seiya's gentle gaze almost makes my heart skip a beat. He stares at the hand he hit me with, a look of deep concern on his face.

"I should go wash off whatever weird germs you gave me."

"…?! I don't have any weird germs!"

I want to punch him right in his stupid mouth, but I can't…! I won't! I am a goddess!

*   *   *

After pulling myself together, I cast the spell opening a gate twenty meters away just to be careful. I peek out from the shadows of the item shop to see what Chaos Machina is doing. She stands in the center of the town square with her giant sword to Nina's father's throat. There isn't another soul in sight. Perhaps everyone is afraid for their lives. Only Nina cries by her father's side. After an exaggerated yawn, Chaos Machina mutters:

"Hmm… Ten minutes is a little long, isn't it?"

Her tongue playfully pokes out from between her lips.

"All righty, enough of that rule. I'm changing it to five minutes, which means time's up. This guy's a goner."

As Nina screams even louder, I impatiently shake Seiya's shoulders.

"H-hurry! She's going to kill him!"

Right as I start to rush out of the shadows to Nina…

"Wait."

Seiya stops me. He already has his sword unsheathed, and he's raising it at middle guard by the time I turn around.

"Wh-what are you doing?"

"Stand back."

What does he plan on doing from this far away?

I take two steps backward, then look at him again. Out of nowhere, the air around his sword distorts.

"Wind Blade!"

Suddenly, Seiya swings his sword horizontally in Chaos Machina's direction from a distance of twenty meters. The distortion shoots out of the sword and soars ahead.

Is this some sort of aerial slash skill that uses air itself as a blade?! D-did Seiya even have a move like that?!

The Wind Blade moves with lightning speed toward Chaos Machina, but since it's so low to the ground, it creates a cloud of dust along the way. Immediately noticing this, she dodges by lightly stepping to the side. However, the ground by her violently bursts open. Chaos Machina looks down the trail to find us and laughs.

"Hee-hee-hee-hee. I knew you'd cooome. What was that, though? You run away and then try to stab me in the back—what kind of chivalry is that?"

"You have no right to speak of chivalry."

I lash out at the coward for taking hostages. However, she simply laughs in amusement.

"It's too bad your surprise attack didn't work. You completely missed me."

"…I wasn't aiming for you."

Seiya and I proceed forward until we are standing face-to-face with Chaos Machina. Nina and her father hug behind us.

"Papa! *Sniffle.* I'm so glad you're okay! Waaah!"

"Th-thank you so much for saving my life!"

Without even turning around, Seiya waves his hand, shooing them away. As if no words are needed, the father bows before picking up Nina and running off into the distance.

"Oh, so thaaat's what you were trying to do. I see, I seeee. Yep. You got meee."

Even after realizing we'd prioritized the hostages' safety, Chaos Machina just laughs…but she completely changes her tune after taking a good look at Seiya.

"What…? What happened to you in these past few minutes? You're like a different person."

Her bloodred eyes lock onto Seiya.

"Unbelievable. Your attributes exceed even mine. What's going on…?"

I speak up in the midst of her bewilderment.

"Oh, so you can use Scan, too? Heh! Seiya's stats are pretty impressive, huh? Well, consider this your last chance to give up!"

I feel so good that I almost want to yell *Serves you right!* but this euphoria doesn't last long. Chaos Machina confidently smiles as if nothing has changed.

"I guess I'll just have to power up a little, toooo!"

"Huh?"

"Release…!"

A jet-black aura begins flowing from her body as a bloodred demon crest appears on her forehead.

"Hee-hee-hee. Did you think you were about to wiiin? Awww, that's too baaad! But I'll let you in on a little seeecret. True masters of war always keep an ace in the hole."

I-I've got a really bad feeling about this! When I finally muster up the courage to use Scan…

CHAOS MACHINA

LV: 66

HP: 5,511   MP: 227

ATK: 1,128   DEF: 1,199   SPD: 1,060   MAG: 517   GRW: 653

Resistance: Wind, Water

Special Abilities: Magic Sword (LV: 18)

Skills: Demonic Curse

Personality: Cruel

Wh-what?! Her attack, defense, and speed all exceed 1,000 now! Even her HP is substantially higher! A-after all that…!

"Now then, how about we have some *real* fun? What do you say, Herooo?"

In a flash, Chaos Machina brandishes her giant sword and then charges at Seiya with blinding speed.

"S-Seiya!" I yell at almost the exact moment the sword swerves toward his neck. However, Seiya is perfectly prepared. He leans his upper body back, completely evading the strike. My relief is short-lived, though.

"Don't get too comfy! I'm just getting warmed up!"

Chaos Machina swings her gargantuan blade as if it were only a twig, trying to cleave Seiya in two. I can only watch with bated breath as she slashes and thrusts, but her weapon does not reach him.

"Hmmm? So it seems you can keep up with me. You have pretty good intuition, don't yooou?"

She briefly pauses her rampage, then creates some distance between them. I get the taste of victory in my mouth.

Y-yeah! This isn't a game! Having higher stats doesn't necessarily mean you'll win! Intuition, strategy—a lot of factors go into fighting!

"Hmmm… How annoying. So, so annoying. But I guess you can never be too careful…"

Chaos Machina spins her sword like an umbrella while addressing me.

"Hey, Goddess, you saw my status, riiight?"

"Yeah, I did! So what?"

"Allow me to show you my skill Demonic Curse."

I—I remember seeing a skill with that name!

I yell out to Seiya:

"Seiya! Watch out! She's going to use a special ability!"

When I alert him, Chaos Machina raises her sword to middle guard, then reverses her grip for some reason.

"Huh?!"

I'm at a loss for words. The blade of Chaos Machina's giant sword now points toward her own stomach.

"It's been so long, so long, so looong since I've shown a human this... I'll let you in on another secret while I'm at it. True masters of war always keep a *second* ace in the hole..."

And then she plunges the blade deep into her abdomen and splits her stomach wide open! Black blood gushes out from the wound like sludge.

"Ahhh!!! Wh-wh-what are you doing?!"

"This is...the Demonic Curse. Hee-hee-hee... Hee-hee-hee-heeee! This overwhelming power...shall bring death to the Hero...!"

She heaves a ragged cough, and more black blood spills from her mouth. The light in her eyes fades as if she was dead, and her head droops.

"Wh-what just happened?!"

Chaos Machina doesn't move, but there seems to be some activity down by her gaping wound. Suddenly, massive arms burst out of her stomach. The ink-black appendages tear the stomach open even wider before trying to pull something out from inside.

"Oh my—"

My heart is in my throat. It's a sickening sight. Even though Chaos Machina is almost the same size as me, a creature around three meters tall comes crawling out of her innards. It has a head with two horns, fangs visible due to the torn mouth, a well-muscled jet-black physique, a long tail, and black wings.

There's no mistaking it. The creature that stands before us now is an incredibly large demon.

CHAPTER 7
Completely Sick

"So this is…Chaos Machina's true form!"

It feels like I'm being engulfed by the deformed creature's sinister aura.

I—I need to calm down! Looks can be deceiving, after all!

I use Scan…and my eyes nearly fall out of my head as I gawk at the coal-black demon's stats…

GREATER DEMON

LV: 66

HP: 15,100   **MP: 424**

ATK: 3,577   **DEF: 3,229**   **SPD: 3,847**   **MAG: 548**

Resistance: Fire, Wind, Water, Earth, Poison, Paralysis

Special Abilities: Full MAG←→ATK Conversion (LV: 15), Flight (LV: 10)

Skills: Demonic Delete

Personality: Cruel

…My legs begin quivering.

Th-th-this has to be some kind of mistake! These stats…surpass those of Demon Lords in D-ranked worlds!

I'm overcome with despair. Our already slim chance of winning vanishes completely. Only a minute ago, I was starting to believe that having higher stats doesn't necessarily guarantee victory…but that's only when the gap between each fighter's attributes is reasonable. Seiya's attack, defense, and speed are all under 1,000. Chaos Machina's stats, on the other hand, exceed 3,000 in all three of those categories. It doesn't matter how good someone's intuition is or how exceptional their fighting intellect is. If their speed is one-third of their opponent's, then they'll get hit—without fail. To put it simply, if Seiya gets hit, he's going to die.

Chaos Machina— No, the Greater Demon creases her golden eyes at me as if she's noticed how pale I've gotten.

"Do you get it now?! The difference in our abilities is obvious! You cannot defeat me!"

Her alluring voice has been replaced by a guttural growl. She raises the knifelike claws of her right hand high into the air.

"Just one attack! All it will take is one attack to separate your head from your shoulders!"

Then she lowers her body to the ground before immediately kicking off with a powerful *boom*! In the blink of an eye, she's right in front of Seiya with her arm raised high over her head!

I have to shut my eyes. What kind of goddess would want to watch her Hero get murdered?

I'm sorry, Seiya. You were truly talented. Unfortunately, it appears that even the Demon Lord's subordinates in this S-ranked world have powers that rival the Demon Lords of D-ranked worlds. I never even dreamed this would be such a frightening place. I never stood a chance of saving it…

Despair, regret, resignation… I open my eyes—and I'm stunned. Seiya is still standing, calm as ever. Not only does he still have his head, but there also isn't a single cut on his body. He just looks bored…like he always does.

"Y-you dodged that?! H-how?! That's impossible!"

Chaos Machina is just as surprised as I am. Standing before a mysterious force, she seems to be hesitating to make her next attack. I use this time to speculate.

H-how did he do that?! That wasn't an attack you could just use your intuition to evade!

…That's when it suddenly hits me. I think back to when Seiya saved Nina's father using Wind Blade. That skill—I thought I must have missed something when I looked at his status earlier. But what if I didn't? What if Seiya used a move not mentioned on his status screen? That could mean only one thing! The stats that Chaos Machina and I saw using Scan are not his actual attributes! To put it simply…

He must have the special ability Fake Out!

I glance at Seiya. Then I focus all my divine powers into my eyes before using Scan. However, instead of his status, I see a sentence:

No peeking.

Wh-what in the world…? Oh…! If the ability Scan is on a lower level than Fake Out, then his status will be blocked from being viewed! B-but at least this proves that he's actually using Fake Out! I strain my eyes and concentrate even harder. Another sentence pops up.

I said "no peeking." That means you, Rista. Peeping's a crime, you depraved voyeur.

Ack! He even specified me by name! H-he knew this was going to happen?! Wait! Who are you calling a "depraved voyeur"?! Now you've done it! I'm going to look at your stats even if it kills me! Time to raise Scan's level!

I pour all my power into my eyes.

Come to me, Goddess Power! …Wait! Waaahhh! My eyes…! They burn! They burn…!! My eyes feel like they're going to pop out of my head! F-fight it! Fight it, Rista! You can do anything you put your mind to!

The moment I release all my divine powers, I hear a crack like shattered glass in my head. It looks like I finally broke through Seiya's Fake Out. As I try to catch my breath, I take a glimpse of his real status screen.

SEIYA RYUUGUUIN

LV: 37

HP: 51,886   MP: 8,987

ATK: 11,005   DEF: 10,369   SPD: 9,874   MAG: 4,787   GRW: 563

Resistance: Fire, Ice, Wind, Water, Lightning, Earth, Poison, Paralysis, Sleep, Curse, Instant Death, Status Ailments

Special Abilities: Fire Magic (LV: MAX), Explosion Magic (LV: 5), Magic Sword (LV: 7), EXP Boost (LV: 11), Scan (LV: 15), Fake Out (LV: 20), Flight (LV: 8)

Skills: Atomic Split Slash, Hellfire, Maximum Inferno, Wind Blade, Phoenix Drive

Personality: Overly Cautious

…Whaaaaaaaaat?! Wha—? What…? What the hell is thiiiiiiiis?! His attributes are five, no, ten times better than when I last checked! Is that even possible?! He has more special abilities and skills as well… Hold up! There is no way he could have raised his stats this high in such a short amount of time! So what the hell is going on?! Has he been using Fake Out ever since his first training session? Wait. But does that mean he was already stronger than Chaos Machina when we first met, yet he still ran away because he wanted to be extra-careful?! Then he went back to the Summoning Chamber to train even more?!

I gaze at the man before me while violently trembling, even more than when I first saw the Greater Demon's stats.

He's sick…! This man is completely sick!

But unlike me, the Greater Demon seems to be psyched up. She spreads her black wings before soaring high into the air. Before long, she stops and roars:

"Well then, allow me to show you something that you won't be able to evade! I'll concentrate all my mana into my fist and crush you with my ultimate attack—Demonic Delete. The village will be turned to ash along with you, but—"

But the Greater Demon pauses...because Seiya is no longer standing there. That's when she notices *Seiya floating right next to her*, and her eyes fly open.

"Wh-what?! You can use Flight?!"

While the Greater Demon stares at Seiya in utter astonishment from her position in the sky, I can't help but trash-talk a little bit. (Not out loud, of course.)

General Chaos Machina, you're strong. Unbelievably strong. You are a true master of war, thoroughly prepared for battle, even hiding two trump cards. If it was any ordinary Hero, you would have crushed him, and it would have been over. But...your opponent is out of your league. I mean... I mean...

Seiya perfectly matches her altitude while brandishing his sword. Its blade burns bright with flame. The high-level ability Magic Sword has been triggered.

As the Greater Demon's face skews at the sight of the Magic Sword, Seiya chants:

"Let my burning blade reduce all to ash... Phoenix Drive!"

The astounding speed of Seiya's strikes leaves a blur in the air, and in an instant, glowing red lines illuminate the Greater Demon's body like a grid. She freezes. Then Seiya sheathes his sword before floating a short distance away. The countless lines on her body glow even brighter, followed by an explosion so powerful, it leaves my ears ringing. Bathed in the scorching winds of the blast, I think to myself:

Okay, seriously... This Hero is overpowered, but he's overly cautious!

CHAPTER 8
An Explosive Final Attack

Charred bits of Greater Demon rain down from the skies. The discarded corpse of Chaos Machina also turns to dark ash and crumbles away. After the Hero majestically descends from above, I rush over to him.

"Seiya…!"

As he looks back with his trademark apathy, I leap in his direction and throw my arms around him.

"…What, are you trying to strangle me?"

"Of course not! I'm just so happy! I mean, I thought this world was done for!"

I yell in excitement, then bury my face in his chest. The steel armor gets in the way, but I can still feel Seiya's warmth.

Sniff! Sniff! Oh no, he smells so nice! Oh man! That's the stuff! *Sniff! Sniff!*

"Quit it. Get off me. You're going to give me whatever strange illness you have."

"No! I am not going to stop!"

I'm not going to lose no matter how many rude things he says. In fact, I'll even give him all the illnesses I have! I hold him tightly in my arms with that thought… I don't have any illnesses, of course.

After enjoying the moment, I loosen my arms and look up at him with a pout.

"But, Seiya…! I'm still a little angry with you! You knew the ability Fake Out, but you didn't tell me. How long have you been hiding that from me?"

Seiya lets out a sigh as he speaks.

"If my attributes were completely visible to an ally such as you, then that would mean that the enemy could see them, too. The first time I met you and went into the Summoning Chamber, I thought to myself, *I need to do something about this*, and started training. Not long after, I learned the ability Fake Out."

As I thought—he was already hiding his real attributes after his first training session.

I force a pitiful expression and gaze at Seiya.

"I get that you don't want the enemy to know your true power, but, like, you could have at least told me. You even blocked me from seeing and left a message telling me not to peek. It kind of hurt my feelings. I mean, we're partners, you know?"

He makes a somewhat sorrowful expression.

"Even if you kept your mouth shut, if there was a monster that could cut your brain open and read your memories, then they'd know my stats. I was just being extra-careful."

"That's so scaaary! You better protect me so that never happens!"

I tightly squeeze Seiya in my arms once more.

"A goddess wouldn't die from that. There's no need for me to protect you."

"Nooo! Protect meee!"

"Get off me unless you want to be chopped into pieces."

I don't let go even then. The moment Seiya instantly killed the Greater Demon is burned into my mind. He was so cool then, just like a real Hero. Just thinking about it makes my heart race.

Wearing a cheerful smile, I look up at his chiseled profile.

Tee-hee. He can't even bring himself to talk. Is he embarrassed? He may try to act cool, but he's still young, after all!

But that's when I realize it. Seiya's lifting up his chin as if to tell me to look behind me.

"Huh…?"

I turn around to find dozens of villagers surrounding us—staring at us in silence.

"Hyaaah!"

Taken aback, I immediately step away from Seiya. Then the villagers begin talking as if they were waiting for this moment.

"Hero! Thank you, thank you for saving our village!"

"Thank you so much for slaying that scary demon!"

Men and women of all ages shower us with cheers and applause. I can even hear some women start to whisper:

"What a handsome man…"

"He's so tall and charming…"

The female villagers seem to be captivated by Seiya's good looks. There's even someone who gives us a freebie from her shop.

"Hello! My name's Jaimie, and I make a living selling fruit. Please take these! I hope you'll enjoy them!"

Lips curled upward, I accept the orange-colored fruit from the young, simple man with dark-brown hair. Before long, a slightly plump man pushes through the crowd, grinning ear to ear.

"Allow me to introduce myself! I am Graham, the mayor of this town! I would like to invite you to my estate for a welcome party."

"A welcome party! What do you think, Seiya? Should we go?"

I flash him a smile, but he shakes his head.

"No. There's still work to be done."

Wow! What a disciplined Hero Seiya is! I bet he already wants to go to the next town so he can save the world! I'm really starting to fall for him!

But in true Seiya fashion, he quickly betrays this notion. He unsheathes his sword and begins using it like a broom to sweep the Greater Demon's ashes into one place.

"What…what are you doing?"

"Just in case."

Seiya aims his left hand at the ashes, then says…

"Hellfire!"

A torrent of flames gushes out of his hand, surprising not only me but the villagers as well. I even hear some scream, "Whoa! That's hot!" They must have gotten caught up in the scorching back draft. Everyone immediately steps away from Seiya.

As if taking that as a signal, he puts even more power into his flames.

"Hellfire... Hellfire... Hellfire... Fire, fire, fire, fire, fire, fire, fire, fire."

A gigantic pillar of flame stands in the center of the town as he continues to chant. But having already reached my limit, I yell:

"What do you think this is, some kind of festival?! Enough already!"

But Seiya doesn't stop. He meticulously continues burning the ash.

"She's one of the four generals of the Demon Lord. She might be able to regenerate if there's even a single cell left! I must reduce her to nothingness!"

"S-Seiya, that's enough! Besides...look around you. You're scaring the villagers. She might be a general of the Demon Lord, but there's no way she's coming back from *that*!"

"...That should do it."

Seiya's magical onslaught finally comes to an end.

Phew, it's over...

...or so I thought. Seiya aims both arms at the powder that remains.

"Time to end this... Final attack: Maximum Inferno!"

An almighty burst of flame, even more powerful than Hellfire, shoots out of his hands and strikes the fine powder like a snake strikes its prey, culminating in a catastrophic explosion. The devastating flames scorch the land, creating trails of fire ten meters around the ash.

"What the hell do you think you're doing?!"

Momentarily forgetting that I'm a goddess, I lose my filter again. I mean, who uses their final attack on a pile of ash?! Is he insane?! There has to be something wrong with his brain!

...For a second, I thought he was cool. I was so excited, I hugged him. I seriously almost saw myself falling for him. But I forgot... This guy totally has a screw loose.

The high-level explosion magic turns the town of Edona into a burning hellscape.

"P-please stop! The fire's spreading to my shop!"

"It's hot! So hot! Somebody help me!"

"H-hey, look over there! Jaimie's fruit shop is on fire!"

I see that the young man who gave us some fruit is now rolling on the ground on fire, so I violently shake Seiya's shoulders.

"STOP, STOP!! JAIMIE'S ON FIRE!!"

But he doesn't stop. I let go of Seiya the Rampaging Ifrit and rush over to Jaimie. I'm able to put out the fire on his clothes with several smacks. Then I cast healing magic on his back to treat the burns.

...A short while later, after I finish healing Jaimie, I turn around and see that Seiya is *still* burning the ash as if his life depended on it.

"SEIYA, STOPPP!!! How much longer are you going to keep that up?!"

Completely ignoring my yelling, Seiya eyes the small pile of ash like a hawk with its prey in sight.

"It's not enough! I can't relax until it's completely gone!"

Eventually, even the mayor begins shouting pleas at Seiya.

"Please... Please just go! Leave this town...! I beg of youuuuuu!!"

CHAPTER 9
Before the Journey

"What were you thinking?!"

On the outskirts of Edona, I vent my anger on Seiya. After thoroughly eliminating the charred ash from this world, our only rewards were the resentful gazes of the townspeople. Unable to stand the awkward silence, I force a smile and push Seiya from behind until we're far away from the town square.

"They were thanking us, and you ruined it! You went from Hero to Demon Lord in the blink of an eye! A little kid even threw a rock at me!"

Seiya's expression doesn't carry a hint of remorse. With a distant tone, he murmurs:

"I saved them all from Chaos Machina. The people of this world seem rather inconsiderate."

"You're the one who's inconsiderate! Jaimie caught on fire thanks to you! Look at the fruit he gave us! It's completely burned! We can't eat this!"

"Not my problem."

He briskly continues ahead.

I can't believe him! The town literally went up in flames because of him, and he still has the nerve to act like that! What did I ever see in him?! I mean, yeah, he's superhot, but his personality is trash!

Frustrated, I approach the town exit until I hear someone running our way. I turn to find Nina and her father. Catching his breath, the father bows to us.

"I-I'm so sorry about what happened. You worked so hard to save our town, but you ended up being ordered to leave. I think everyone was just surprised because of all the fire…"

I shake my head, letting him know it isn't his fault.

"We brought this on ourselves. I mean, we burned a shop…and a person."

Actually putting it into words depresses me. This isn't what a Hero does. This isn't even what a sane person does.

"A-anyway, I wanted to thank you for saving us! I'm so glad I caught you before you left!"

Nina's father hands a pouch to Seiya.

"It's not much, but I hope it helps!"

When Seiya, who had been looking away the entire time, peeks into the bag, his eyes light up.

"Oh, money. It's always good to have money to buy items and equipment. I'll take it."

"S-Seiya! You're a Hero, remember? Show some modesty."

However, the Hero places a silver coin in his palm, then furrows his brow.

"Hmm… There's less here than I thought. I'm sure you've got more than this. Empty those pockets."

"…?! That's not what a Hero does! Now it looks like you're mugging him!"

I yell at him, but Nina's father reaches into his pocket with a wry smirk and pulls out some change to hand to Seiya. Nina then sends me an innocent smile.

"Ha-ha-ha! He may be sick in the head, but he's a good person! That much I know!"

I place a hand on Nina's shoulder and somehow manage to force a smile.

"Well, Nina, you're half-right. While he is sick in the head, he is definitely *not* a good person."

"Excuse me? I am not sick."

"A mentally stable person wouldn't set people on fire and extort money from others! Ugh! I'm so embarrassed! Come on—we're going to the next town!"

After bowing to them, I swiftly take Seiya by the hand and begin walking. I hear Nina yell out to us from the background.

"Thank you, nice lady! Thank you, sick man! Thank you sooo much!"

"N-Nina! Don't say that!"

Even after being scolded by her father, Nina continues waving good-bye with a huge smile on her face. Never having been more embarrassed in my life, I say good-bye to the town of Edona.

After walking in silence for a good while, Seiya tries to stuff the money he received in his pocket. Glaring at him from behind, I notice something fall from his chest.

…It's the pressed flower Nina gave him.

"Wow, Seiya, you still had this? Didn't you say this was a cursed item that attracted enemies?"

"I thought about it and came to the conclusion that that would be advantageous. It's a lot easier to control a situation when the enemy makes the first move."

"…Mm-hmm, sure."

"What?"

"Oh, nothing."

I have no clue what he's thinking. He's unpredictable. But…well, whatever.

After my anger subsides, I pull myself together and put a cheerful note in my voice.

"Come on—let's hurry to the next town! According to the information Great Goddess Ishtar gave me, we should arrive at Seimul if we keep heading north. Your first ally should be there! Oh, I can't wait!"

However, Seiya stops in his tracks, then clearly declares:

"No thanks. It's too soon for that."

"What?! Wh-wh-what do you mean 'too soon'?!"

"I'm heading back to the spirit world."

"You've got to be kidding me! Why?!"

"Why else? To train."

"Seriously?! You're going to go train in the Summoning Chamber *again*?!"

"Yes. After giving it some honest thought, I'm positive that once the

Demon Lord learns that I've defeated General Chaos Machina, he's just going to send someone stronger. I should prepare before arriving at the next town, just in case."

"You're probably right about the Demon Lord eventually sending someone stronger, but with stats like yours, I can't imagine them being much of a threat."

"Don't make assumptions. There's no guarantee that I'll win next time, so I have to make sure I'm always at my best until then."

"B-but if we don't go to the next town, you won't meet your next ally, and you won't be able to buy stronger equipment. Don't you think that's a problem?"

Seiya places a hand on his chin in deep thought.

"It would be nice to have new weapons and armor. Can't you just make them? You made my bed in the Summoning Chamber, after all."

"My divine powers to create can only be used in the spirit world. Naturally, it's also prohibited to bring anything I make there to another world. Giving humans excessive help goes against the laws of the gods."

Seiya frowns.

"You're useless."

"What?! How dare you! I'm an excellent supporter! You saw my healing magic! I completely healed Jaimie's burns after you set him on fire!"

"I could've done that with a medicinal herb. In other words, your value to society is only around medicinal herb level."

"Don't compare me to a medicinal herb!"

"At any rate, I'm returning to the spirit world to train. If you have a problem with that, you can go to the next town by yourself."

"G-going to the next town without you would be pointless. What are you even saying...?"

"Then hurry up and open the gate to the spirit world, herb woman."

"F-fine... Wait! What did you just call me?!"

CHAPTER 10
The Divine Blade

"...So I see you're back again."

"He is seriously way too cautious. I mean, he's paranoid—sick, even."

Once again, I complain to Aria in her room. There are many different goddesses in the spirit world; some of them are straight-up rude, but Aria is always so nice. She's been nice to me ever since I came into being. If Great Goddess Ishtar were my mother, then Aria would definitely be my older sister.

Robed in a sexy dress with her cleavage exposed, Aria elegantly sips her tea like always. I sneak a peek at her—what I assume to be—G-cup breasts and bite my lip in frustration. She never fails to arrest the attention of any male god who crosses her path. I mean, I'm a D-cup, and I'm sexy in my own way, but still...

She's better looking than me and more experienced. Everything I can do, she can do better.

It can't be helped, really. She was born in the unified spirit world thousands of years ago and has saved countless worlds with the Heroes she summoned. She's a seasoned goddess. And then there's me: a rookie goddess who's been around for only a little over one hundred years with barely five worlds saved under my belt.

"*Sigh.* I want to hurry up and save Gaeabrande so I can become a high-ranking goddess like you, Aria."

"You shouldn't look up to me."

"What are you talking about? You've summoned Heroes to three hundred worlds, and you saved every single one of them! You're a legend!"

I try joking with Aria, but I can detect a hint of sorrow in her smile.

"I didn't save all of them."

I did hear there was a world even Aria couldn't save. But...

"It was just one world out of three hundred, right? You can't save 'em all."

As I smile, Aria's expression turns grim.

"It's not that simple, Rista. For the people who lived there, it was the only world—the only life—they had. They don't get another chance. You can't just say, 'You can't save 'em all' and move on to the next one."

"N-no, I understand that. I get it, but...I still think it's amazing that you only failed one time out of three hundred."

Aria faintly shakes her head.

"It was a B-ranked world. It wasn't a difficult mission, but...I made a mistake... This is my cross to bear, and I must carry it with me for the rest of my life."

"U-uh..."

I try to get back on topic to lighten the mood.

"B-by the way, that overly cautious Hero of mine has been in the Summoning Chamber all day since we've been back! Can you believe it?"

"...More weight training?"

"Yeah! The meathead basically lives to work out!"

As I continue breezily, Aria's sweet smile returns.

Phew... Looks like she's feeling a little better...

Aria holds her empty teacup and stands.

"I'm going to have some more tea. Would you like some, Rista?"

"Oh, sure. Thanks."

...That's when the door flies open with a bang.

Taken aback, I look over and only grow more surprised...because Seiya is standing there in his loungewear! Even Aria is surprised. The moment she sees him, she drops her teacup, and it shatters on the floor. However, Seiya is indifferent and looks at me.

"There you are. I was looking for you."

He casually approaches me, and I scream.

"S-Seiya?! This is a lady's room, you know! Get out! I mean, look what you did. You scared Aria and made her break her teacup."

"I-it's fine... It's really okay, Rista..."

Then Aria walks over to Seiya, her eyes glistening.

What the...?! Did Aria fall for his good looks, too?! D-don't be fooled! That's all he has going for him! If he lays one finger on her, I'm going to kill him! That womanizer! No, that *goddessizer*!

In the midst of my rage, Aria passionately gazes at Seiya.

"So you're the Hero Rista summoned..."

"Who are you?"

A look of disgust flashes across Aria's face as if she was stunned by Seiya's discourtesy, but she almost immediately clears her throat and wears her usual smile rich in compassion.

"I am Aria. The Goddess of the Seal, Ariadoa. What brings you here?"

Seiya appears to hesitate as if unsure whether he wants to say anything to a goddess he just met, but he eventually speaks up in a calm manner.

"I'm not leveling up as much as before no matter how many sit-ups or push-ups I do..."

Seiya seems troubled, but I'm screaming for joy in my head.

Yes! The gains from his weight training have finally started to dwindle! Heh-heh-heh! He'll just have to level up from fighting monsters now! Which means we can finally start our journey!

I put on a serious expression before saying anything.

"Seiya, this is just how things are. There is a limit to how far you can go with weight training alone. So how about we go to Gaeabrande and start fighting monsters?"

"Actually fighting monsters, huh? It's too risky."

"No...it's pretty much the standard for any Hero..."

"Instead of fighting monsters, can't you just create some heavier dumbbells and tougher training equipment for me?"

"N-no...! Absolutely not! No, no, no! That's nothing more than a stopgap!"

"Then what should I do...?"

Seiya is at his wits' end for a change. Seeing him distressed like this makes it hard to yell *Go fight monsters, stupid!* without feeling awful.

That's when Aria pipes up, as if unable to watch anymore.

"Seiya, hypothetically speaking…how would you feel about undergoing training from a god or goddess here?"

Her proposal takes me by surprise.

"A-Aria?! Wh-wh-what's gotten into you?!"

"He wouldn't have to worry about being killed by a god in the unified spirit world. Plus, he would receive many more experience points than he ever would from a monster. Hee-hee… It's a little trick of the trade."

Aria winks. Seiya gives a nod that suggests he's completely on board.

"I see. That's not a bad idea."

"A-Aria! Can I have a word with you over here?"

I call Aria to the window side and whisper in her ear.

"Are you sure you should be promising him that?! I mean, is it even possible to train under a god?!"

"It won't be a problem. I'll grant him permission and tell Ishtar beforehand."

"B-but who in the world is even going to train him? I'm the Goddess of Healing, and you're the Goddess of the Seal. Neither of us are suited for fighting."

Aria smiles while pointing at the window.

"What about the god who's always training over there?"

Outside her window is the unified spirit world's vast, magnificent garden. A god practices sword techniques around the gracefully sculpted fountain.

He's a stubborn god. Other gods berate him, saying that he's ruining the beautiful view with his sword practice, yet he doesn't stop.

He is Cerceus, the Divine Blade.

Aria walks toward the door.

"I'm going to go ask Cerceus if he'd be willing to help."

I drop my shoulders, then let out a deep sigh.

Sigh… The dream of finally starting our journey once again slips through my fingers.

And so we head to the garden to meet Cerceus.

The moment he sees us, he pauses his training and gives us an awkward smile. An intimidating individual, Cerceus is built like a god on all fronts—tall and well muscled with short hair that's accented by his mustache and goatee.

"Well, if it isn't Miss Ariadoa, Ristarte, and...oh? Is that a human?"

He knits his brows.

"A summoned Hero, yes? It would be for the best if you humans refrained from roaming around the unified spirit world."

Just as Seiya's about to say something, Aria takes a step forward.

"Cerceus, I have a request. I would like to know if you could train this Hero."

A few moments of silence go by until...

"I wouldn't mind doing a favor for a high-ranking goddess such as yourself. However..."

Cerceus slowly approaches Seiya and scowls.

"Human, are you prepared to train under me? It's not going to be easy, and there is no guarantee that your body can even handle it."

His awkward smile transforms into a smug grin as he sizes up Seiya, but Seiya doesn't even bat an eyelid and speaks in his usual tone.

"Oh, you've got guts, but don't come crying to me when you reach your limit. I won't let you quit."

Cerceus flinches.

"H-hey. Why does it sound like you'll be the one training me? That's my line."

"Enough chitchat. Meet me in the Summoning Chamber when you're ready. Got it?"

"Y-yeah, sure...... Wh-who *is* that guy?!"

After Seiya turns and begins to walk away, Cerceus soon rushes after him in a fluster. Just watching this sends a chill down my spine.

H-how did he reverse their roles like that?! Seiya Ryuuguuin—what a terrifying man! B-but Cerceus isn't called the Divine Blade for nothing! He's going to humble Seiya! Then he'll finally start behaving himself and maybe even actually become a decent Hero!

...I actually believed that once upon a time.

CHAPTER 11
Rigorous Training

On the first day, Seiya and Cerceus enter the Summoning Chamber together.

As always, I was told not to come in until he buzzed me, so I decided to respect his wishes and leave them alone. However, around noon, I found Cerceus having lunch by himself at a table in the dining hall. I take a seat by his side and timidly ask:

"Hello, Cerceus. How's Seiya doing?"

Immediately, he opens his mouth wide and cackles.

"Mm! He has a lot of fight in him. He's not all talk after all! A lot tougher than I expected! There aren't many who can keep up with me from day one!"

"R-really?!"

"But he still has a long way to go if he wants to beat me, though!"

Seeing him in such a good mood relieves me. It looks like they're getting along really well.

"Thank you so much! Please keep up the good work!"

I bow to Cerceus before leaving the dining hall.

Wow! It really sounds like everything's going well! Good job, Seiya!

Then day two comes around.

I find Cerceus in the dining hall at around noon again, but this time he has a rather glum look on his face as he pokes the fish on his plate with a fork. I take a seat next to him once more and say hello.

"Hello again, Cerceus. How's training?"

"G-great. W-we're working hard."

...Huh? Why is he stuttering?

Cerceus heaves a deep sigh.

"Tsk. He's gotten awfully strong in a mere two days."

Seiya's EXP Boost ability was already over level 10 last time I checked, so that's likely what's contributing to his growth period. Even though this is something to be thrilled about, Cerceus mutters disdainfully:

"If only I could unleash my true powers..."

"Yeah... We deities can't use one hundred percent of our power on humans, after all..."

"And that's the problem. With the exception of special cases, our powers are greatly suppressed due to the spirit world's rules. I'd probably be able to defeat him if I was able to use my real powers..."

"Excuse me? Come again?"

"N-nothing! Don't worry about it!"

Did he just say he'd "probably" be able to defeat him?! Did Seiya already surpass Cerceus?! But it's only been two days... No, I must have been hearing things! There is absolutely no way that happened.

"A-at any rate, he makes a good rival! Wah-ha-ha-ha! *Cough! Wheeze!*"

It looks like he was laughing so hard that he started to choke. Seeing the Divine Blade act differently from yesterday gives me a touch of anxiety.

Then comes day three.

Cerceus is sipping on some water in the dining hall. He doesn't look so good, especially with those sunken cheeks.

"Cerceus, have you lost weight?"

The Divine Blade speaks with a touch of lethargy...

"No... I'm fine..."

"Oh, I'm glad. Uh... So how's Seiya doing?"

"Oh, y'know..."

"Is he progressing?"

"So-so..."

"What do you mean by 'so-so'?"

"Y'know, so-so means so-so."

"Sure, but, like, could you be a little more specific? He is my responsibility—"

He slams his fist against the table before I can finish.

"Enough!! Give it a rest!! I'm on my lunch break right now!! Stop talking about training!"

"Eek! S-s-sorry!"

Our yelling attracts the attention of the other gods in the dining hall. Not wanting to be the center of attention, Cerceus calms himself...

"Sorry. I shouldn't have raised my voice."

And with those words, he wearily plods out of the dining hall.

Day four. Cerceus isn't in the dining hall during his lunch break. He hasn't looked so well lately, so maybe he's getting some rest in his room? Pondering to myself, I make Seiya something to eat in the spirit world kitchen, since he locked himself in the Summoning Chamber. As I head to the corner of the kitchen to get the seaweed for the rice ball...

"Ahhh!!"

I scream on instinct. Crouching over a mat next to the seaweed is Cerceus.

"Cerceus?! What are you doing here?!"

"Shhh! Quiet!"

"I-is something wrong? You almost look like you're hiding from someone."

He motions for me to come closer, then has me squat before whispering into my ear.

"Ristarte, listen carefully. That Hero of yours...is sick."

I don't have the heart to tell him I know that already. I just listen in silence as he wears a pale expression and speaks in a trembling voice.

"I told him that his training was complete, yet he insists he needs more and won't let me go. To tell the truth, I've been training him with next to no sleep since day one."

"O-oh, so that's why you look so exhausted..."

"Even after I told him that he's already three times stronger than I am, he said he wouldn't be able to relax until he's at least a hundred times stronger than me. There's something wrong with him—he makes berserkers look cute. A super-berserker is what he is."

In the middle of his frightening tale...

"Hey."

Cerceus and I slowly look up in the direction of the deep voice. There, standing firm with his legs apart and his arms crossed, is the super-berserker himself.

"Uwaaa!"

I can't help but scream.

"Ooo-eek!"

Cerceus, though, lets out a cry unlike anything ever heard before.

"Cerceus, lunchtime is over. What are you doing sitting next to seaweed?

"Oh, I, uh..."

He seems to be at a loss until a ray of hope flashes in his eyes.

"Oh, right! I was sitting here...pretending to be seaweed!"

Even I am amazed.

"Pretending to be seaweed?!" I've never heard a more bizarre excuse in my life!

But Seiya chooses not to pry, simply giving Cerceus a cold stare.

"Is that right? Well, are you finished?"

"N-not yet. I'm going to need some more time to really *become* the seaweed and—"

"No. We're leaving."

Then Seiya grabs him by the neck and mutters to himself:

"Taking into account the time we just wasted, we're going to have to train for the rest of the day without any more breaks."

"N-no more breaks...?"

Cerceus is trembling in fear.

"Noooooooooooooooooo!"

I am stunned to see him loose a howl of terror.

"Cerceus! You're breaking character!! Get it together, man!!"

"I'm sick of swords! I never want to see another sword again!"

"Whaaaaaat?! The *Divine Blade* is tired of swords?! What's going on here?!"

"I hate them! I hate those stupid elongated strips of metal with their pointy ends!"

"He's not even calling them 'swords' anymore?!"

Seiya pays no heed to Cerceus's childish tantrum as he drags him out of the kitchen by his neck.

"Somebody heeelp!"

While watching him being taken away with tears in his eyes, I plead:

"S-Seiya! Quit it! He doesn't want to go!"

That's when the door to the kitchen opens, and Aria comes rushing over with her face burning red.

"Rista! There you are! Ishtar has been looking all over for you!"

"What?!"

Judging by how worked up Aria is, it's clear this is serious.

"Cerceus! Please put up with Seiya just a little longer!"

I say my good-byes...

"You can't leave me like this! Noooooooo!"

...and I leave the kitchen and head to Great Goddess Ishtar's room, leaving Cerceus's screams to trail off in the background.

CHAPTER 12
Ready to Go

"Pardon the intrusion."

When I walk into the room, Ishtar is seated in a chair and wearing a warm smile as she knits. It would be extremely rude of me to say, but she is the perfect embodiment of a sweet old lady in this moment. She speaks to me with her usual comforting tone.

"Ristarte, how is your Hero's training with the Divine Blade coming along?"

I first apologize for the special treatment we're receiving.

"I'm really sorry about all this. Not only has Seiya remained in the spirit world, but he's also being trained by a god…"

"It isn't a problem. Of course, this is the first time a Hero has ever requested guidance from the Divine Blade rather than fighting monsters. However, this is still within the range of assistance. It doesn't violate our divine rule against excessively helping humans. This is simply the first case."

"O-okay…"

"So is Seiya Ryuuguuin's training progressing?"

"Um… About that… He actually made Cerceus want to quit, saying he never wanted to see another sword again or something."

"Hoh-hoh-hoh," Ishtar laughs.

"Cerceus was a timid man when he was a human, after all."

"Wait! He used to be a human?!"

There are two types of gods: those who originally came into being in the unified spirit world and humans who did countless good deeds and were reincarnated as gods. I assumed Cerceus was the former, but...

"Yes, Cerceus was once a knight. Of course, those memories disappeared when he became a god. However, things engraved upon one's soul rarely ever change. Being forced to undergo such harsh training must have awakened this weak side of his. But, well, this ended up being a good learning experience for him."

Th-the training was supposed to be for Seiya, though...

Incidentally, in the past, I once asked Ishtar if I was the type of goddess who came into being in the unified spirit world or if I used to be human, but she politely dodged the question. *"I will tell you when the time is right,"* she'd said. But the more I think about it, there isn't much of a difference between the two types, since former humans don't remember anything of their past lives anyway. Ever since then, I stopped caring.

Ishtar places her knitting on the table, then looks at me with a gentle gaze.

"Now, Ristarte. Unfortunately, I didn't call you here today to chat. I am sorry to tell you this in the middle of your Hero's training, but you need to go to the next town immediately."

Since I was eager to get this show on the road ages ago, I waste no time answering.

"Okay!"

But then I start to wonder...

"W-wait... Did something happen on Gaeabrande?"

Her expression was grim by the time I noticed.

"Originally, the starting village I chose for the two of you was a relatively safe place. However, the Demon Lord sensed that we had started to take action, and it appears that the next town is already in imminent danger."

Ishtar has the ability to see slightly into the future. The accuracy of her visions puts my goddess intuition to shame, so whatever she says is happening is happening.

"Although time in the unified spirit world moves more slowly, I need you to embark on your journey right away. Ristarte, can you do that for me?"

"Of course! Right away! I'll leave right now!"

After departing from Ishtar's room, I walk determinedly through the spacious sanctuary.

He can complain and grumble as much as he wants, but I'm taking him with me even if it's the last thing I do!

I shove open the door to the Summoning Chamber.

"Seiya! We're going to Gaeabrande! ...What the—?!"

I struggle to make sense of the horrifying sight. Seiya is mounting Cerceus and raining punches on him.

"Oof! Gwah! Ow! Urgh!"

Cerceus guards his head with his hands while groaning.

"H-hey!! What do you think you're doing?! Stop that!"

Seiya finally stops after I rush over.

"Seiya! Why are you torturing Cerceus like that?!"

Confronted by my rage, he feigns ignorance.

"What are you talking about? This is part of our training."

"Oh...is that right...?"

I was taken aback because it looked like Seiya was beating the tar out of him...b-but I guess that was silly of me. He would never do something so mean...

I smile at Cerceus as he lies on his back.

"I was really worried for a second! That sure didn't look like training."

"..."

But he doesn't say a word and keeps his hands over his face.

"...?! Cerceus isn't saying anything! Were you two really training?!"

"Why are you here?"

"Oh yeah! I almost forgot!"

I get straight to the point.

"Gaeabrande is in trouble! We have to leave right now! I know you're probably still training, but I'm taking you with me!"

Seiya wipes his sweat with a towel.

"Fine by me. I have nothing left to gain from training with this guy anyway."

Cerceus sits, burying his face into his knees without saying another word. Ignoring this, Seiya gallantly dons his steel armor, then brushes back his glossy black hair.

"I'm perfectly prepared. Come, the next town awaits."
"Sure… But… At least give Cerceus a proper apology before we go!"

I cast a spell, creating a gate that will take us right to the outskirts of the town Seimul. With this method, I can instantly travel anywhere in Gaeabrande that Ishtar scouted for me beforehand. Personally, I wish we could have started somewhere a little farther away from town so that we could fight monsters and gain experience points, but we can't afford to be picky right now.

Seiya and I step into Seimul and immediately witness people rushing out of town in a panic, carrying their household furniture and goods. I grab one of the fleeing men and ask him to tell us what's going on.

"Krain Castle in the northwest was attacked by an army of undead and got destroyed! It's only a matter of time before the monsters come to this town! Get out of here while you still can!"

After the man runs off, Seiya turns to me with a question.

"Hey. What are undead?"

"Undead are monsters that are essentially moving corpses. You can think of them as zombies if that helps. By the way, it's really difficult to stop them with just punches and sword strikes alone."

"Oh? Then what kind of attacks are effective?"

"Fire magic. The item 'holy water' is effective as well."

"Holy water, you say? Then let's go to the item shop first."

According to Ishtar, Seiya's first ally will apparently be waiting for us at the church in town, so though I'd like to go straight there, it probably would be helpful if we had some holy water to fight the undead.

"Okay, but let's make it quick."

We jog until we find the item shop and run inside.

*   *   *

A portly shop owner stands behind the counter of the narrow building.

"Thank goodness someone's still here."

"Ha-ha-ha! Of course I'm still here! My business is everything to me, after all!" the owner says with a chuckle.

"You're here for holy water, right? You're going to need it for the undead, and you can never have too many. Make sure you stock up, traveler."

Seiya nods while pulling the pouch full of money out of his pocket.

"I'll do just that. Give me one thousand."

The shop owner grimaces.

"…I know I said you can never have too many, but there really is a limit, and I think it's around a thousand—that's definitely way too many. For starters, although holy water is kept in small bottles, you're not going to be able to carry that many. Even if you could, you would be so weighted down that you wouldn't be able to move. Plus, my shop doesn't even carry that many to begin with."

"You don't have enough? And you call yourself an item shop? Make an order for a thousand. Now."

"I-I'm so sorry! We'll take ten! Ten should be plenty!"

I order the holy water on Seiya's behalf.

"…This isn't nearly enough."

Seiya still seems to be in a sour mood even after leaving the store, but I ignore him and hurry to the church. A short distance away from the item shop is a church with massive double doors that creak when I push them open. Down the long red carpet are four people standing before an altar: a priest, a nun, an animated-looking boy dressed in silver armor with dark-brown hair, and a girl clothed in a robe with a curly red side ponytail. After they acknowledge us, the priest looks at me with tears in his eyes.

"How divine! Even in your human form, I can tell! You are a goddess, correct? We have received enlightenment from the gods and have been waiting for you two here!"

He points at the boy and girl.

"These two are descendants of the dragonkin, and they shall journey with you to defeat the Demon Lord!"

The short girl with red hair quickly lowers her head, but the brown-haired boy arrogantly places a hand on his hip.

Descendants of the dragonkin…! These two kids are going to become Seiya's new allies!

I can't wait to talk with them… However, my goddess intuition begins violently ringing alarm bells in my head. It's impossible to describe with the five senses that humans have, but I can sense the squirming of rotting flesh. I can't tell which one of them it is, but…

I whisper to Seiya.

"Be careful, Seiya. I've got a bad feeling about this. I'm pretty sure one of those four is undead."

"Hmph. I'll handle this."

"W-wait. Seiya…?"

He snorts, then starts approaching the four at the altar.

CHAPTER 13
Unwelcome Surprises

Being quickly advanced on by Seiya, the white-haired priest respectfully bows.

"Oh, Hero! I apologize for not introducing myself! I am Marth, a priest—"

While the old priest Marth is introducing himself, Seiya takes some holy water out of his pocket and pours it on the man's head without even warning him.

Sploosh... Sploosh... Sploosh... Sploosh...

"...What...?"

The priest is dumbfounded as the holy water drips down his head. Then comes the usual shriek of terror.

"S-S-Seiya?! What are you doing?!"

It's not me who's panicking, though.

"Wh-what do you think you're doing?!" the young boy of the dragonkin yells.

"Why is he pouring holy water on him?!"

The young girl's eyes also open in surprise just as the last of the quartet reacts to the spectacle.

"Father Marth!!"

The nun places a hand over her mouth as if she may faint. It's understandable, though. Who wouldn't be shocked to see someone perform such a barbaric act on an elderly man they just met?

But one person yells even louder than the rest—the one who had holy water poured on his head, Father Marth.

"Gwaaaaaaaaaaaaaaah!"

He lets out a roar an old man should have been incapable of producing. Soon, smoke begins rising from the priest's head.

Huh?! Wait… D-does this mean that…?!

"H-hey, hey!"

The young boy seems to have figured it out as well.

This is the reaction you get when you pour holy water on the undead!

"S-seriously?! Does this mean the Hero knew he was undead from the very beginning?!"

"Wh-whoa! Amazing!"

Even while the two kids gasp in admiration, the undead disguised as a priest continues tearing at its head in agony.

But before long, the undead looks this way—its face inflamed as if burned by the holy water. Its vile laugh echoes through the church.

"Geh-heh-heh-heh! Impressive, slayer of Chaos Machina! I was planning on killing all of you together the moment you let your guard down, but you got me!"

Then it lowers itself into a half-seated position as if to lunge at us.

"But it's not a problem! I'll just kill you all now with the immortal powers I received from General Deathmagla of the Demon Lord's army! Prepare to die!"

"B-bring it on, asshole!"

The young dragonkin boy draws his sword.

"Heh! Don't forget about me!"

The young girl raises her mage staff aloft. Instead of joining them in battle, though, the ever-so-careful Seiya strikes up a conversation with the nun for some reason.

"How long has that priest worked at this church?"

"H-he came to this town two days ago from Krain Castle as a missionary…"

"I see. So he isn't originally from this town…"

"S-Seiya! Now's not the time to be making small talk! Help them fight!"

"It's been taken care of. I've already neutralized the enemy."

"Huh?"

As soon as he says that, the undead priest's head, arms, and legs crumble, falling onto the church's floor. After rolling across the ground for a few seconds, its head finally realizes what happened to its body and screams.

"Whaaaaaat?!"

Seiya calmly observes the priest.

"It doesn't bleed even after having all its limbs removed. It's not even hurt. I see. So this is an undead."

The two dragonkin descendants' eyes bulge.

"B-but how...?"

"I—I didn't see him unsheathe his sword..."

Not even I saw what happened—even with my dynamic vision, which surpasses that of a human's. Seiya must have gotten a lot stronger during his training with the Divine Blade. I really have to check out his status as soon as possible.

"Hey, Seiya, just tell me this one thing: How did you know that Father Marth was the undead one?"

"My reasoning was simple."

"Would you be so kind as to explain this reasoning of yours?"

"I suppose. The first clue was that the priest was the oldest, feeblest one here. In short, he pretty much looked undead already, so I decided to pour the holy water on him."

"O-oh... Wait! *That's* why you chose him?! What kind of rationale is that?!"

Some might say his reasoning was half-assed, while some may say what he did was inhumane. Some may even call it elder abuse, but the fact of the matter is that he was right. I decide to overlook the rest.

The undead head rolls around on the floor while yelling out in frustration.

"D-dammit! Don't get so cocky just because you defeated me! General Deathmagla's army destroyed Krain Castle and is heading to this town as we speak! Geh-heh-heh-heh! That's ten thousand undead soldiers! Surprised? When they arrive tomorrow morning, this town will be reduced to ash! Enjoy the rest of your short lives!"

T-ten thousand undead soldiers will arrive tomorrow?!

I shiver in horror, but as always, Seiya is completely unfazed and nods after the undead priest finishes talking.

"Well, I've gotten all the information I wanted out of it. Time to clean up. And since it's undead, I'll need to be even more careful than usual…"

The instant his words reach my ear…

"Everyone, run!"

I scream, shoving the young dragonkin and nun from behind.

"Huh? Why do we have to run? I mean, the enemy has been immobilized."

"That's not the problem! What happens next is the real issue!!"

"Wh-what do you mean?"

"Listen, that Hero right there actually unleashes his full powers after the battle is already over, when he's 'cleaning up.' Urgh! See—what did I tell youuu?!"

An ear-piercing blast echoes in the background. Seiya must have used explosion magic. The second I open the church doors, the high-level magic's blast wave blows us outside. The explosions sound off again and again while flames burst from the shattered stained glass windows. It is only a few minutes before the church of Seimul comes crumbling down.

"Th-the church… Seimul's historic church…! Ahhh!"

Witnessing the downfall of the house of worship, the nun feebly falls to her knees and faints. Meanwhile, out of the fire appears the Ifrit himself, and the first words out of his mouth are:

"There is no need to worry. The monster is gone."

"So is the church! The nun even passed out!"

Once again, Seiya completely ignores my criticism. That's when the boy wearing silver armor timidly approaches him.

"W-well…you're kinda weird…but there's no questioning your strength. All right, you pass."

He extends a hand to Seiya to shake.

"Nice to meet you, Hero! I'm Mash, warrior of the dragonkin!"

Up next, the girl with the curly red side ponytail and mage robe greets Seiya as well.

"Heh-heh! I'm Elulu! I grew up with Mash in the same village, and I'm a dragonkin mage! I'm looking forward to working with you!"

The friendly girl Elulu approaches Seiya in his silence.

"Hey, what's your name?"

"...Seiya. Seiya Ryuuguuin."

While introducing himself, Seiya has the audacity to drizzle holy water on Elulu's head.

"Hey!"

Startled, she jumps.

"Hmm... It appears she's human."

Seiya nods to himself before pouring holy water on Mash's head as well.

"H-hey! The hell do you think you're doing?!"

"This one's human, too."

He even pours some holy water on the unconscious nun's head.

"Perfect. All human."

"Give her a break... She's not even conscious..."

After my criticism of Seiya for obvious reasons, he pours holy water on my head as well.

"Heeey! Why me?!"

"You could have been switched out with an undead when I wasn't paying attention."

"Do you seriously believe there was enough time for that to happen?!"

Watching our exchange...

"J-just how little trust does this Hero...have in other people...? He's way too cautious!"

"Y-yeah... He's sick..."

Mash and Elulu seem put off by Seiya. It doesn't help that he's now staring at them without saying a word.

"Wh-what are you looking at?"

"Y-yeah, what? Why are you just glaring at us like that? It's creepy!"

That's when it hits me. Seiya's using Scan on them, isn't he? O-okay, then! Guess I'll take the opportunity to check their statuses myself!

My eyes glisten like Seiya's as I stare at them.

"Eek?! The Hero and goddess are scaring me!"

Elulu yells and starts tearing up. Nevertheless, I focus everything on my eyes, and before long, I am able to see their statuses.

MASH

LV: 8

HP: 476   MP: 0

ATK: 206   DEF: 184   SPD: 101   MAG: 0   GRW: 28

Resistance: Poison

Special Abilities: ATK Boost (LV: 3)

Skills: Dragon Thrust

Personality: Brave

ELULU

LV: 7

HP: 355   MP: 195

ATK: 98   DEF: 160   SPD: 76   MAG: 189   GRW: 36

Resistance: Fire, Water, Lightning

Special Abilities: Fire Magic (LV: 4)

Skills: Fire Arrow

Personality: Optimistic

...Oh. They're a lot more...average than I expected. They're not even one-hundredth of Seiya's skill level. I figured they'd be stronger, since they're of dragonkin blood. B-but I guess they'll get stronger with time?

While trying to think optimistically, I glance at Seiya to my side and a chill immediately runs down my spine—because he's glaring at them with the most intense look I have ever witnessed.

CHAPTER 14
Breakdown

"Hey! How long do you plan on staring at us, weirdo?!"

Standing before the church ruins, Mash screams at Seiya. After finally averting his gaze, Seiya bitterly frowns before saying:

"Yeah… No thanks."

"…Huh? What did you just say?"

"I said no thanks. I don't need you two. Your attributes are too low. You're useless to me."

"E-excuse me?! I dare you to say that again, you bastard!"

Ever the strong-willed youngster, Mash flies into a rage, but Elulu manages to put on a smile.

"Ah…ah-ha-ha-ha! W-well, we're still developing, after all! So we'd really appreciate it if you could think of things in the long term. Okay?"

However, Seiya just glares back at the redheaded girl.

"By the way, your fire magic is just a weaker version of mine. It's completely useless."

"Completely useless?! H-how mean!"

"And you're 'still developing'? I have to wonder just how useful two kids, who didn't even notice that the priest they were hanging out with was undead, will grow up to become."

Frustrated, they clench their teeth, unable to argue. I can't not say something after all that.

"C-can you blame them, though? That priest completely blended in so no humans would notice. It's only natural that they didn't—"

"That's not what I'm talking about. I'm saying that their ability to sense danger is low. Being with them would put me at risk. To put it bluntly, they'd just get in the way."

As if unable to take any more, Mash spits on the ground.

"Hey, Hero, don't get carried away and start looking down on people just 'cause you're a little tough."

He gets in Seiya's face and scowls.

"Don't you dare judge me based on my attributes alone! You wanna throw down?! Wanna see what I'm really made of?! I don't care if you're some god's chosen Hero or whatever! They didn't call me the Hero Mash at Nakashi village for nothing!"

"Very well. It should only take me a second to show you the difference in our abilities."

In an attempt to calm the explosive situation, I stand in between Mash and Seiya.

"G-guys, relax! Especially you, Seiya! You've been extremely rude to Mash! Apologize!"

"Why? I have no reason to apologize."

Seiya looks at Mash like one would regard a pebble by the roadside.

"I'll say it one last time. I don't need you. Now go back to Namaste village."

"'Namaste'...? N-no, it's Nakashi—! Ugh! You ass! That's the last straw!"

Elulu latches onto Mash before he can hurl himself at Seiya.

"Mash, no! Fighting isn't the answer!"

"Shut up! Get off me!"

I whisper to Seiya, leaving Mash to Elulu for the moment.

"H-hey, Seiya, listen. According to Great Goddess Ishtar, there are sealed places we can't get to without the dragon crests on their hands. What I'm trying to say is, we're not going to be able to save Gaeabrande without them."

"So you're telling me I should bring them along as keys instead of allies?"

"Well, I guess you could think of it that way for now..."

A desperate measure for a desperate situation—I needed to somehow convince him to take them with us. However, there is one thing I didn't notice: Mash had broken away from Elulu's grip and was listening to our conversation behind us.

"Keys?! So now we're just items to you?! Is that it?!"

"N-no! That's not what I meant!"

Oh no, oh no, oh no! I just poured oil onto the fire! H-how am I going to fix this now?!

I start panicking, until…

"Mm…!"

I turn in the direction of the suppressed voice to find huge teardrops running down Elulu's cheeks. Then, like a dam bursting open, the very next moment, she wails hysterically.

"Waaaaah! 'Useless'? 'Keys'? Enough alreadyyy! I've been training really hard since the day I was born! Why do you have to be so meeeeeean?!"

"Y-yeah, I know…! I know how you feel, so please don't cry, Elulu!"

"Hmph. What is this, a day care? Ridiculous."

"Seiya, shut the hell up for one second!"

A Hero who looks the other way, a crying young girl, a boy gnashing his teeth…

Ahhhhhh! When did everything get so messed up?! This is the worst! W-wait! I'm a goddess! It's my duty to fix this!

I look around, trying to find a solution, until I eventually see a group equipped with heavy armor approaching us. I point.

"O-oh?! What's this?! Guys, look! Someone's coming this way! I wonder why!"

Perfect! We can finally change the mood……or so I thought. My joy is brief. Five knights stop before us with solemn expressions. They each speak up in turn.

"They told us there was some sort of trouble at the church, but…what happened here?! It's completely burned down!"

"Look over there! Nun down!"

"Hey, you there! Explain yourselves! What happened here?! Depending on how you answer, we might have to take you back with us!"

Uuugh! Why me?! Things are even worse now!

"Oh, this? Ah-ha… Well, you see, it's actually a funny story—"

Right as I'm trying to concoct an excuse, the nun wakes up.

Oh, come on!!! Things can't possibly get any worse than this! If they find out that Seiya was the one who destroyed the church, we're all going to jail!

But contrary to my expectations, the nun backs us up.

"Oh, knights… To tell you the truth, an undead disguised itself as a priest. If it wasn't for these people, I would have been killed."

"S-so the reason the church was destroyed was because…?"

"Yes… My head is still a little fuzzy, so I can't quite remember all the details…but…I'm sure the undead set fire to the church and destroyed it."

She stammers with a serious expression, as if trying to remember what happened. It doesn't seem like she's lying on our behalf. Perhaps she convinced herself that the undead burned down the church, unable to believe that a Hero would commit such heresy.

"However, there is one thing I clearly remember. The undead priest said that an army of ten thousand undead will be arriving at this city by tomorrow morning."

"Wh-what?!"

"T-ten thousand…?! Impossible!"

"I heard the undead army that destroyed Krain Castle is moving south… but I had no idea it was so huge!"

The knights are taken aback by the nun's report. However, the nun smiles.

"There is nothing to fear. God has not abandoned us. These people are proof of that: a goddess who descended from heaven to save Gaeabrande, a Hero who has received divine revelation, and two child descendants of the dragonkin—the legendary race that has been protecting Gaeabrande since ancient times."

The knights' eyes light up when they hear our introductions, and there is a stir among them. The old knight with a goatee bows to us.

"Please accept my humblest apologies! We are the Roseguard Imperial Knights! We were dispatched as an advance team to Seimul, territory of the empire, to protect the town from the undead! Please forgive us for our rude behavior earlier!"

The five knights all bow to us in unison.

"Oh, Hero! Please…! I beg you! Save us from the undead army!"

Unusually, Seiya steps forward and talks to the oldest knight.

"How much will you give me if I destroy that undead army?"

"Excuse me...? G-give you...what?"

"Money. What else would I be talking about?"

"Seiya?! Is now really the time to be asking about money?! You're a Hero, not a mercenary!"

"I learned a new skill recently, but I need a decent amount of money to practice it."

What...? A new skill? What kind of skill requires money?

"O-of course, you will be graciously rewarded by the empire once your task is complete. You should expect a few thousand gold pieces at the very least..."

"Is that so? Then I'll need that in writing. I'm going to make sure you pay the amount I deserve."

With a smile, the knight offers reassuring words after signing the contract Seiya forces on him.

"The rest of the knights should be arriving shortly! While not much, two hundred imperial knights will be fighting by your side!"

However...

"Yeah...that won't be necessary."

"Whaaat?! You don't want our help?!"

The knights are baffled by his sudden reply.

"B-but..."

"I don't need your help. There are still many people who haven't left town, correct? Stay behind and protect them."

Seiya turns his gaze away from the puzzled knights and looks at Mash.

"Hey, you. Mushroom from Namaste village."

"You can't be serious... It's *Mash*! From *Nakashi* village! Get it right, asshole!"

"Shut up and answer me. Can you do anything about this situation?"

"Wh-what does that even mean?"

"I'm asking what you can do against ten thousand undead soldiers."

"I—I..."

He pauses and the dragonkin duo exchanges glances. Seiya then gives it to him straight.

"Listen and listen well. There isn't a single thing either of you can do that will help in this situation, but it won't be a problem for me. Now return to Namaste village."

"Stop calling it Namaste village! And we're not going back!"

"Then stay with the knights and protect the town. You can at least do that, right?"

Flustered, Elulu checks in with Mash.

"M-Mash, what should we do? Want to protect the town?"

"Shut up! Like hell I'm taking orders from that guy!"

Mash then turns on his heel.

"I've had enough of this! We're gonna take matters into our own hands!"

"M-Mash! Wait!"

"H-hey…! Mash?! Elulu?!"

But Mash ignores me and continues walking away. Elulu then gives me an apologetic bow before chasing after him.

After parting ways with the knights, Seiya and I wait on the outskirts of town together.

"Hey, Seiya… You don't think Elulu and Mash are going to try to fight the undead army alone, right?"

"They're not that stupid. Besides, I'm going to destroy that entire army before they have a chance to do anything. There is nothing for you to worry about."

I shoot him a reproachful glare.

"You're going to 'destroy' them? There's nothing they can do to help, but it won't be a problem for you? Listen, you're extremely strong. You even became a better swordsman by sparring with the Divine Blade Cerceus, right? But things are different this time around. You're outnumbered. There are ten thousand undead coming. Ten thousand. You should understand this more than anyone. Seiya, it's not too late. Let's go ask the knights and Mash and Elulu for help."

"I don't need them."

"Ugh! Seiya! What happened to the old you—the abnormally cautious you?! I thought you'd be relieved to have even one ally!"

"Having an extra hundred or two allies against ten thousand undead won't make a difference. Besides, those dragon kids and the knights aren't immortal deities like you. They don't need to die meaningless deaths."

Wh-what…? I feel like I just heard something…unusual. Is Seiya worried about those kids in his own way?

I stare at Seiya in wonder…and am immediately met with a surprise. Seiya begins floating in the air. I-is this the ability Flight?!

"S-Seiya?!"

He glances down at me from above.

"By the way, I don't need you, either."

"…Excuse me?!"

"They said the undead were moving south, so I'm going to go north. Wait for me at the town's inn."

And just like that, Seiya soars off, leaving me alone on the outskirts of town.

"Th-this can't be happening… He even said he didn't need me—a goddess? A-am I dreaming…?"

After standing there in shock for a few moments, I explode with rage.

Th-that selfish, arrogant little…! I'm not going to let him get away with this! Seiyaaaaaa!

I scream into the air:

"Order!"

Then I offer a prayer to Ishtar in the unified spirit world.

"Please grant me the ability Flight."

Deities' powers are greatly limited when we descend to the human world in human form—for we are bound by the law that we're not allowed to help humans too much, even if it's to save their world. However, there are exceptions. During emergencies, the restrictions can be eased for the sake of supporting the Hero. That's what Order is: an emergency measure in the spirit world for unlocking the goddess's true powers. Of course, to do this, we need permission from Ishtar. However, I am requesting only the ability Flight this time to catch up with Seiya, so I should be able to get permission pretty quickly…

As expected, as if I have a fever, I feel my back begin warming while radiant white wings suddenly appear.

Hee-hee. It's been a while since I've had these! What beautiful wings, if

094   THE HERO IS OVERPOWERED BUT OVERLY CAUTIOUS   VOL. 1

I do say so myself! That Seiya, I bet he thought I couldn't fly. Well, just you wait! Once I find you, I'm going... I'm just going to wing it! Heh.

"Rista Wiiing!"

I spread out my wings like a swan and take to the skies, heading after Seiya as he slowly shrinks into the distance.

"Don't you dare underestimate a goddess!!"

CHAPTER 15
One Versus Ten Thousand

Flying at full speed, I finally start closing in on Seiya, who looked like an ant only moments ago. It seems I have the advantage when it comes to flying. In actuality, his Flight ability wasn't even at that high of a level when I checked his status before, compared to my level 14. If I put it in kilometers per hour, I'd be able to fly anywhere from sixty to eighty kmh. I catch up with Seiya in no time.

"I've got you now!"

…I try grabbing him from behind, but he evades.

Tsk! Those reflexes! It's like he's got eyes in the back of his head.

"What, you followed me? I told you I don't need you."

"Hmph! What's your problem? I've got the upper hand while flying, you know? So you better watch what you say unless you like eating dirt!"

Seiya shrugs off my confident remark and mutters to himself.

"All right, that's enough warming up. Time to start flying seriously."

And then he's gone in a flash.

"Um…"

By the time I realize it, he's already leisurely flying dozens of meters ahead.

H-how did he get so fast?! D-dammit!

Wildly flapping my wings, I start chasing after him. Flying is one thing I don't want to lose at. I mean, I have such beautiful wings. Seiya, on the other hand, doesn't have wings at all. He's just floating. I have to beat him no matter what it takes.

But…he's fast! Even though I'm flying at max speed, the gap between us only widens.

Y-you're going down! Raaaaaah! Goddess Power activate! I'll focus all my power into these wings and—owwwwwww!!! My back feels like it's on fire! Ahhhhhh! My wings feel like they're melting! Push through the pain, Ristarte! Don't give up! You're going to be a Great Goddess one day!!!

I give it all I've got, seriously hurting my back and wings in the process. But Seiya fades out of sight in the end. Utterly drained of all energy, I stop midair as I try to catch my breath.

I—I even took the spirit world emergency measure… I can't beat him even with my divine powers…

Depressed, I finally lift my head, only to see Seiya floating in front of me.

"This is why I told you I didn't need you. Ugh. What a pain in the ass. Well, come on. Let's go."

Seiya then grabs me by the wrist before taking off.

…I was annoyed that he left me behind. I was sick of how overly cautious he was from the moment I met him. But while it may have been on a whim—the kindness he showed by waiting for me, his warmth blanketing my wrist—when I look at his chiseled features as his bangs flutter in the wind, it gives me butterflies in my stomach.

H-he's actually really handsome up close! *Hff! Hff!* And he's holding my hand… W-wait a second! I-it's like… It's like we're on a date!

Seiya suddenly looks back at me.

"Hey, Rista."

Oh my—! He said my name for the first time! He usually just yells "hey, you" or something to get my attention!

"Y-y-yes?"

My heart violently races.

I mean, we're flying really high up, so nobody can see us from down below! D-don't tell me that Seiya wants to fool around up here?! W-we can't! We mustn't! Love between goddesses and humans is strictly prohibited! But…well, I guess a little love never hurt anybody. At the very least, a kiss should be okay, right? Yeah, it'd definitely be okay. In fact, I want him to kiss me. Wait. Maybe I should just kiss him?

Letting my imagination run wild, I pucker up like an octopus, when suddenly...

"I'm going to speed up."

"...Huh?"

His grip around my wrist tightens, and I'm dragged off at extreme velocity.

"Gyaaaaah!"

An unbelievable amount of air flies down my throat. I can hardly even breathe properly. While I can't see for myself, I know my face is a disaster right now.

Incidentally, Seiya himself is fine, since he's using his magic to fly, but being dragged through the air like this is pretty awful. To put it simply, if Seiya were sitting in the cozy pilot's seat of a jet, then I'd be outside, tied to one of the wings by a rope. That's what this feels like.

While being battered by the air resistance, I finally come to a shocking realization. The plunging neckline of my favorite white dress is wide open, exposing my bra! I'm even starting to pop out on one side!

"Noooooo! Stop! Wardrobe malfunction imminent!!"

But he doesn't stop, and I continue being dragged through the sky by the arm while my bra hangs on for dear life.

Seiya finally slows down after half an hour or so. After adjusting my dress, I mutter:

"I thought I was going to die..."

"What? Goddesses don't die."

He says this just before looking back. That's when he sees that my hair is a mess, my face is a wreck, and my clothes are in disarray.

"...Have you always looked like that?"

"It's *your* fault I look this way, you jerk! Just look at me! My wings are a disaster! You can even see some skin here and there because we were going so fast, my dress tore!"

"Then use that healing magic you're so proud of. Now be quiet. What are you going to do if they hear us?

I desperately want to give him an earful, but I clam up the moment I look in the direction he's pointing...because a large army of undead advancing through the vast plains of Gaeabrande comes into view.

From around two hundred meters in the air, they look like battalions of ants forming lines, but since I have better vision than humans, I can clearly see them when I strain my eyes. The undead army mainly consists of zombies and skeleton knights. While slow, they steadily advance south.

"S-so what are you planning on doing? Don't tell me you're going to charge them..."

Without answering, Seiya takes me by the arm once more.

"We're not high enough."

"What?! We're going to fly even higher?!"

As we ascend straight up, I glance down. The already small undead army is getting even smaller.

I wonder how high we are. By the time Seiya finally comes to a stop, the enemy just starts to look like a moving black inverted triangle.

"Hmph. They're marching together to intimidate through numbers. It's an impressive sight, but it's also foolish. I would have spread them out to avoid risk because a bombing would wipe them out in an instant."

"T-true, but bombs are a thing of your world, right? There aren't any fighter planes or bombs in this world."

"But I suppose the powers I gained are more or less equivalent to the destructive force of fighter planes and bombs."

Seiya then raises his arms into the air before closing his eyes.

"...Keep quiet."

I wait in silence for a minute before a shadow suddenly passes over.

Huh? Wh-where'd all this shade come from?

When I look up, I'm so shocked that I almost forget to continue flying...

...because a colossal object is now floating overhead.

"Wh-wh-wh-what is that?!"

"Meteor Strike!"

At his call, the meteor roars as it descends from the sky. It passes right by us—well, with a hundred meters of distance in between.

"It's a small meteor with a radius of only a few dozen meters, but the energy it possesses from falling at such a high speed is incredible. It will probably annihilate the army of undead in one shot."

Before I can even say anything, the shining meteor proceeds to crash into the marching inverted triangle of undead, followed by a deafening explosion! The flames rise like fireworks.

It really was less of a meteor crash and more of an outright bombing. The awesome thermal power swiftly transforms the fields containing the undead into a blazing inferno.

"I adjusted the falling speed of the meteor for the undead. A slow collision would have only made a crater, but a rapid descent creates a phreatic explosion by raising the ground temperature to an ultrahigh degree upon impact. At least one square kilometer of land was affected."

"W-wow...!"

That's the only thing I can say as I stare at the sea of flame spreading beneath us. I mean, this man seriously defeated an army of ten thousand all by himself! And he did it by altering a small meteor's orbit to land where he wanted it to. Only a high wizard can use extremely high-level magic like that!

"While powerful, it's a spell with many restrictions. You can only use it in open areas with no people, and you need silence and some time to concentrate in order to cast it. It's not very practical overall."

"B-but how did you even learn a spell this powerful?"

"Back in the Summoning Chamber, when I had Cerceus in the mounted position while I practiced my melee strikes, I had a vision. And that vision turned into Meteor Strike."

O-oh! That's when I walked in on them! Wait a second... He was training with the Divine Blade, but that's not even a sword skill! Ah, whatever. That's beside the point. More importantly...

Gazing at the scorched plains, I think to myself.

I do feel bad for Mash and Elulu, but the difference in level between them and Seiya is staggering. Honestly, this Hero could probably save Gaeabrande by himself.

"I think I destroyed around ninety percent of them, but I'm a little worried... I should cast it one more time just in case," Seiya casually remarks before raising his arms back into the air to prepare for another Meteor Strike. The corners of my mouth curl up in secret.

Heh-heh-heh… Ha-ha-ha-ha! Perfect! This is too perfect! I bet that General Deathmagla or whatever his name was died in the blast, too! Seiya might be a little off, but his talents really are one in a billion! Hey, maybe we can even use Meteor Strike on the Demon Lord's castle and just get this over with! Ha-ha-ha! This is going to be a cinch!

I get so carried away because of Seiya's godlike powers that I completely forget just how frightening this S-ranked world Gaeabrande can be. Unfortunately, I will soon receive a painful reminder…

…and it will come at a price.

CHAPTER 16
A Blade's Reach

After landing the second meteor, Seiya seems to stagger a bit in the air.

"S-Seiya? Are you okay?"

"I used too much MP. I need to rest a little."

"All right, let's return to Seimul and head to the inn."

He draws his brows together as if in agony. I've never seen him like this. It's understandable, though. He just used an extremely powerful spell twice in a row. Never mind his MP—he must be mentally exhausted as well.

Seiya groans.

"I had 15,000 MP...and now...I only have...13,500 MP left..."

"...! You have plenty left!"

"Don't be stupid. We would be in trouble if an enemy attacked right now."

"I—I don't know about that... Are you sure...? A-at any rate, let's get you to the inn."

On the one hand, I'm sick of his overcautious personality, but on the other, I'm blown away that he had 15,000 MP. And so we fly back to the town of Seimul.

By the time we're back in town, numerous Roseguard Imperial Knights have already gathered. The older knight from earlier comes rushing over when he sees us.

"I'm so glad you're okay! How did it go?"

I tell them exactly what happened.

"Th-they were wiped out...? All ten thousand undead soldiers...? A-are you sure? Of course I am not doubting you, but..."

The knights put on uncomfortable smiles while exchanging glances. It seems it's still hard to believe that an entire army of undead was defeated within a few hours. No matter how much of a Hero you are, such a task should be incredibly difficult. Seiya pulls out the signed contract from earlier and demands his reward. However, the knights stammer that they'd like to confirm firsthand before hopping on their horses and galloping out of town. Then, as if to avoid any further discussion, the older knight notes that we must be tired and guides us to the inn.

It all started on the third morning during our stay at the inn.

In my own private room next door to Seiya's, I'm combing my hair when there's a knock at the door.

"Ugh! Are you finally done getting ready? ...Hmm?"

But when I open the door, it's not Seiya. I look down and see Elulu, still dressed in a robe with her curly red ponytail bobbing to the side.

"E-Elulu...?"

She fidgets.

"I'm sorry about the other day, but I really need to talk to you."

"Don't worry about that. Besides, it was our fault. More importantly, what did you want to talk about?"

"Mash disappeared two days ago. I can't find him anywhere."

"Are you sure he didn't go back to your village?"

"He would have told me if he was going to do that."

I place a hand on her shoulder, trying to calm her down as tears well up in her eyes.

"Elulu, it's going to be all right. The undead army is gone, so it's probably nothing serious."

Elulu tries her best to put on a smile.

"Yeah, I heard! It's all the town is talking about. That Hero really is strong, isn't he?"

"You could say that."

"I don't see him, though… Is he in the room next door?"

I let out a deep sigh while explaining.

"Get this—he's been *obsessed* with synthesizing ever since we got here."

Yes, after Seiya received that substantial reward from the knights, he went to the weapon shop and bought every piece of equipment he could get his hands on before locking himself in his room. He apparently wanted to test out his new ability Synthesis. Now I know why he wanted all that money.

"Anyway, let's tell Seiya we're going to be gone for a while. We wouldn't want to hear him complain about it later."

"Huh…? 'We'…?"

"I'm coming with you. Let's go look for Mash."

"A-are you sure? I mean, we're not even your allies…"

"That's just something Seiya said. Besides, as a goddess, I can't ignore people in need."

"Th-thank you so much!"

Elulu smiles from ear to ear. I take her to Seiya's room and knock on the door, but there's no answer.

"Seiya? You're in there, right? I'm coming in."

But when I open the door, Elulu and I are met with a surprise. Dozens of swords and armor are chaotically piled on the floor, almost spilling over. Seiya stares at a sword with great concentration until finally noticing we're there.

"Rista, look at this sword."

Seiya, who usually never shows any emotion, is blushing a little as he shows me the sword. I gaze at the blade with its elegant silvery-white glow and raise my voice.

"I-is that a platinum sword?! W-wow! What in the world did you combine to make that?!"

"I needed to change my perspective. Combining swords with other swords only slightly increased the strength. However, strong weapon synthesis requires something completely different to serve as a catalyst."

"A catalyst? Like what?"

"The hair of a goddess. I found some in your room when you were gone. Then, when I synthesized it with a steel sword, it turned into this platinum sword."

M-my hair…? He was in my room?

I have mixed feelings about it, but I keep my mouth shut until…

"I want to make some spare platinum swords, so could you give me some more of your hair? I'll only need around one thousand strands, root and all."

"Do you want me to go bald or something?!"

I refused, but for some reason, Elulu looks at me in admiration, her eyes glittering.

"Wow! Your hair is magical?! I wish I were a goddess!"

"Hoh-hoh-hoh! Wh-what can I say?"

Right after I allow myself a prideful smirk, there's a knock at the door. I soon hear a familiar voice coming from the other side.

"There's a delivery for you, Hero."

It's the old lady who runs the inn. When I open the door, she's holding something long vertically in both arms, wrapped in cloth, before handing it to me. It's surprisingly light despite its large size, so I'm able to hold it without any help.

"What is it? Who brought it?"

"I don't know what's inside, but a man wearing a hood brought it by. He said, 'Allow me to offer this to the Hero who defeated the undead army.'"

After the innkeeper closes the door, Seiya quizzically stares at the gift.

"I don't trust whoever brought this. It's probably an explosive. You open it."

Just because goddesses can't die doesn't mean he should treat me like a meat shield. Regardless, I unwrap it just like I'm told, unveiling a full-length mirror. It's wider than most. Two people could probably line up in front of it side by side.

"Oh, what a wonderful gift… Huh?"

That's when I notice. It's not a mirror embedded in the wooden frame but a transparent board like glass. When I place it against the wall, I can see the same wall right through it.

"Wh-what in the world is this?"

However, in the very next moment, it starts emitting a sound.

Vshhh.

The transparent board darkens.

"Eek!"

Elulu and I scream.

"Wh-what's going on?"

An ominous image appears on the "mirror." In a dimly lit room sits a person tied to a chair, blindfolded and gagged. The captive's hemp clothes are stained dark red with blood.

Elulu is the first to notice. She covers her mouth, then speaks in a trembling voice.

"Mash...! That's Mash...!

Clink... Clink...

I can hear someone approaching Mash. A man eventually appears by his side and talks to us.

"Can you see me? Can you hear me? I can see you very well. A handsome Hero, a dashing goddess, and a cute red-headed girl."

He's on the shorter side, wearing a black robe like the grim reaper. Bald from the forehead back, with three eyes adorning his grotesque face, it's clear he isn't human. He speaks with a vile tone one would expect from a face like that.

"It's wonderful, is it not? This mirror is the result of the Demon Lord's power. It can display images from two separate places at once like this."

The man suddenly smirks.

"Oops. I forgot to introduce myself. I am Deathmagla, one of the Demon Lord's four generals. I normally use my abilities to re-create human corpses into undead."

I grind my teeth at the revelation.

D-Deathmagla...! So he wasn't marching with that army of undead?!

"That was one impressive performance. You annihilated all my undead soldiers in the blink of an eye. Aether magic, was it? Very powerful. I'm lucky I was controlling those undead from afar."

Deathmagla places a hand on Mash's shoulder, causing him to flinch.

"But, well, even though they were only undead, it still takes a long time to create that many. It really left a bitter taste

in my mouth. I just had to get back at you somehow, and so I did—with this boy."

Elulu is trembling by my side.

"N-no… Th-this can't be happening."

"Oh, we played and played and played. It's really fun playing with a living human for a change. Dead bodies never react no matter how much you prod them, so it gets a little boring, you see."

Deathmagla puts a knife to Mash's throat.

"But I've had my fun, so I'm going to kill him now."

Elulu's scream echoes throughout the room. Deathmagla looks at us with a bloodthirsty gaze.

"Hero, this is all your fault. How dare you employ such a cowardly tactic to destroy my army."

But Mash's murmurs get Deathmagla's attention.

"Oh? Begging for your life?"

After the monster removes the gag, Mash weakly strains his voice.

"Y-yo, Hero… I—I heard you defeated that army of ten thousand…"

Mash raises his voice as if struggling through the unimaginable agony and fear.

"You may be a piece of shit, but you're the real deal! I can't even compare! That's why…"

Tears of blood stream down from under the blindfold.

"That's why…I need you to save the world in my place!"

I hear Mash scream and instinctively look away. I can't watch. I can't listen. Mash knows there's no hope for him. That's why he's entrusting his last wish to Seiya, despite his hatred for him.

Deathmagla looks bored.

"What? So you're not going to beg for your life? You cried like a baby when I was torturing you, but now you're trying to be the tough guy? Nice try, but it's over for you."

Elulu tightly squeezes my arm.

"Goddess! Please save Mash! He's the only family I have! Please…! Please save him!"

I rack my brain, but no matter how much I think about it, it's hopeless. I say nothing. I just stand there in silence. Elulu lets go of my hand, drops to her hands and knees, and bursts into convulsive sobbing.

"No…! No, no, no! Somebody… Somebody save Mash… Please…"

Deathmagla smiles in amusement as he watches us.

"Oh yes. Just remember, while you were able to destroy an army of ten thousand, you failed to save a single human dear to you."

But his face clouds over when he looks back at Seiya.

"My, my. Look at you, Hero—remaining calm even at a time like this. I heard you were quite the cautious one. Perhaps you already discovered where we are and sent someone here to stop me?"

Deathmagla shows his true colors, wearing a fiendish expression and roaring with laughter.

"Gya-ha-ha-ha! But you wouldn't be able to do that! 'Hero'? Don't make me laugh! You're nothing! All you can do is stand there and watch as I slit this boy's throat!"

Even after being peppered with insults, Seiya doesn't flinch, and he whispers into my ear.

"Rista, open a gate to the spirit world."

"O-okay. But…"

It doesn't matter how much slower time moves in the unified spirit world when Mash is going to be killed seconds from now.

"Just open it. That kid…"

As if he couldn't even hear what Deathmagla was saying, Seiya begins speaking calmly to himself like always.

"…Mash the dragonkin, huh? He's got guts. I guess I could let him carry my stuff."

Deathmagla seems frustrated. Did he hear Seiya?

"What are you plotting, Hero?"

"…I've constantly visualized what to do in a situation like this."

"What are you babbling on about? Answer me."

Deathmagla is growing annoyed. Even I don't know what Seiya's rambling about.

"The same thing happened with Chaos Machina. I saw Nina's father on the verge of death through the crystal ball. Ever since then, I've been wondering to myself what I would do in a similar situation but with far less time to work with."

Seiya lowers his posture and places a hand on the grip of his sheathed sword. Deathmagla's three eyes open wide the moment he notices that Seiya is getting into battle stance, and his lips curl into a sinister grin.

"You fool! You're going to attack me? Just because you can see me in the mirror doesn't mean I'm there! You can't hit me! You're too far away!"

Deathmagla then points the dagger at Mash's throat.

"Gya-ha-ha-ha! Time to pay for destroying my army!"

"Noooooooooo!"

Elulu screams. I don't look at Mash, however, but Seiya. The slightly unsheathed part of his blade shines with a brilliant light. In the next instant, he draws his glowing sword at lightning speed and slashes at the mirror horizontally. Immediately, Deathmagla's arm holding the knife spews out blackish blood before soaring through the air. Realizing he's missing an arm, Deathmagla screams.

"Wh-wh-what is this?! It can't be...!"

With his arm still in full swing, the Hero stares down the enemy like a hawk.

"This photon sword tears through the very fabric of space—Dimension Blade!"

CHAPTER 17
Great Goddess

I'm so deeply moved by the miracle that I'm trembling.

Dimension Blade: an attack that can cut through the fabric of space itself… That's… That's amazing! How does that even work?! The Hero's powers are godlike!

As I'm blinded—overcome with emotion—someone tugs on my arm.

Before I realize it, I'm going through the gate to the unified spirit world with Seiya and arriving at the all-white Summoning Chamber.

"Huh?"

I have no idea what just happened; Seiya smacks me on the head.

"Ouch! What do you think you're doing?!"

"Don't space out. The real fight starts now."

"Huh? The real fight…?"

"Dimension Blade only cut off Deathmagla's arm. Once he pulls himself together, he's going to go on a rampage and kill Mash."

"O-oh yeah! What are we going to do?!"

"That's why we came here where time flows one-hundredth the speed of Gaeabrande. If things go smoothly, we'll have around ten seconds before he snaps out of his confusion and picks up a weapon to kill Mash. To sum it up…"

Seiya then walks straight to the Summoning Chamber doors and pushes them wide open.

"Starting now, we have fifteen minutes to find a way to travel from the unified spirit world to where Deathmagla is and save Mash. Got it? Now follow me."

I'm puzzled for a moment, but…

"Y-yes, sir!"

With a loud voice, I reply to Seiya as if I were talking to one of my superiors in the spirit world.

After that, I guide Seiya through the sanctuary as requested until we reach Great Goddess Ishtar's room. I hesitate in front of the door, but he urges me on.

"What's wrong? This is the highest-ranking goddess's room, right? Hurry up and open the door."

Su-sure, Ishtar will be able to find out where Mash is, but…

I give Seiya one final warning before opening the door.

"Listen, Seiya, Ishtar is a really—I mean, *really* important goddess. You *have* to treat her with respect. Got it?"

"Got it."

"I sure hope so. Anyway, leave the explaining to me. Do not say a word."

"Yeah, yeah."

After clearing my throat, I open the gorgeously decorated door. Ishtar is resting in her chair and knitting like she usually does.

"I apologize for bothering you. It is I, Ristarte, the Goddess of Healing. I have come here today to make a request to—"

Seiya upstages me before I can even finish my greeting.

"You're taking way too long. I'll cut right to the chase. Listen, Grandma, we need to find Mushroom in Gaeabrande, so I need you to open a gate that takes us right to him."

"Seiya!! I told you to keep quiet! And stop calling Mash 'Mushroom'! You're making it sound like we're looking for food!"

More importantly, how dare he talk to a Great Goddess like that! For crying out loud, he was saying Mash's name right up until a few seconds ago! But now it's back to Mushroom.

…I feel like I'm going to explode if I don't find an outlet for all this rage. However, Ishtar simply smiles just like she always does.

"Hoh-hoh-hoh. In short, you want me to find your friend, correct? However, excessively helping humans is prohibited by spirit world law…"

"All I need you to do is create a gate at a specific point in Gaeabrande like this woman always does. There's no problem with that, is there?"

"Hmm… I suppose not, if you put it that way."

"I do. Make it quick."

"Yes, yes."

Even though my heart is pounding out of my chest, Ishtar doesn't seem offended by Seiya's incredibly rude behavior. She stands up, grabs a large crystal ball off the shelf, then places her hand on it for a few moments.

"…I see. It appears he is being held captive in an underground vault beneath the forest near Krain Castle."

"W-wow, you're amazing! S-so, Seiya, what's the plan? Should we have the gate take us to an area slightly away from the vault similar to last time?"

"No, things are different from last time. Right in front of the rotting Mushroom will do."

"Right in front of the boy, yes? Very well."

Ishtar casts a spell, creating a gate to Gaeabrande. Around ten minutes have elapsed since we came to the unified spirit world, so we should have plenty of time to save Mash.

I bow deeply to Ishtar.

"Thank you so much! I will definitely repay you for your kindness! Seiya, tell her thanks!"

"Well done. Your assistance was praiseworthy."

"…?! Who the hell do you think you are?! …More importantly, I've got to ask. You do have a plan to deal with the undead, right? Because the moment we walk through that gate, I guarantee that Deathmagla's going to have his zombies and skeletons attack us by the dozens."

Seiya sends me a reproachful gaze.

"Who do you think you're talking to? Of course I'm perfectly prepared."

As Seiya proceeds toward the gate, I see his left hand and my eyes widen.

…I see. It looks like he really is prepared. His left hand is already wreathed in flames.

"I'm going to use Hellfire on him the moment the gate opens. Use that opening to save Mushroom. Got it?"

"G-got it!"

A-all right! I'm gonna give it all I've got!

But when Seiya tries to open the gate—

"…Seiya Ryuuguuin."

—Ishtar suddenly calls his name.

"What?"

"You've grown."

"You make it sound like you've known me for a while, but I believe this is the first time we've met."

Seiya seems baffled for a moment, but he soon nods as if he just had an epiphany.

"Oh, wait. She's probably just senile."

I can't take it any longer.

"Show some respect, you ass! She is *not* senile! She is an all-seeing goddess, and she's complimenting you for slightly improving as a person who would do anything to save his allies despite being overly cautious, arrogant, and rude!"

After furiously berating Seiya…

"Isn't that right, Great Goddess Ishtar?"

However, Ishtar doesn't say a word. She only smiles.

Seiya gives a smug snort.

"I'm not doing anything daring like saving an ally. I'm just going to pick a mushroom. Now come on. Let's go."

We open the gate to Gaeabrande.

"May you be victorious."

I hear Ishtar's kind voice behind me.

CHAPTER 18
Ingenuity

The moment I walk through the gate, Seiya is already extending his left hand, wreathed in Hellfire, toward Deathmagla.

"My hand…! My haaand!!"

Writhing in pain, Deathmagla's screams echo through the dim, needlessly spacious torture chamber.

"…Huh?"

By the time Deathmagla notices the intruders and lays all three eyes on Seiya…

"Burn. Hellfire!"

…he is engulfed by the flames that burst from Seiya's hand.

Y-yes! That was surprisingly easy! I was worried, but there don't seem to be any undead around, either!

Leaving Deathmagla's fate in Seiya's hands, I rush over to Mash and untie him.

"Mash! Are you okay?"

"Y-yeah…"

I promptly remove his blindfold, but after seeing him…I almost instinctively look away. His body is covered in burns, and all his fingernails have been ripped out. Mash notices my reaction and tries to force a smile, but it's a painful sight when so many of his teeth are missing.

A ball of anger rises from the pit of my stomach.

That sadistic three-eyed monster! How could anyone do something so cruel to a young boy, barely even a teenager?!

"Don't worry. I'm going to take care of you right now!"

I cast a healing spell.

I start off by focusing my powers on relieving his body of stress and fatigue along with healing his burns.

In the middle of healing Mash, I figure Seiya's probably about finished, so I casually look over…and I can hardly believe my eyes.

As the flames continue to lick at Deathmagla's flesh, Seiya is furrowing his brow with a pained expression. It's an odd look for him, since he's never one to really show his emotions.

B-but why? Deathmagla is the one on fire…so why?

However, it isn't long before I realize it. While he is indeed cloaked in flames, they're not the crimson flames of Hellfire. Sinister black flames appear to be protecting him from Seiya's skill. After the flames of Hellfire fade, the black flames leave Deathmagla's body and coalesce into a human shape around twenty meters tall.

"Wh-what…what is that thing?!"

Mash struggles to lift his head. The moment he sees the beast of black flames, its face utterly featureless, his body goes into convulsions.

"Th-that's…! That's…! That's…!"

"Mash? Wh-what's wrong? Mash, calm down!"

Mash turns utterly pale as his teeth chatter. Deathmagla wraps his left hand with a cloth to stop the bleeding while glaring at Seiya.

"So that's the fire magic that you so proudly killed Chaos Machina with? Too bad it doesn't work on me. You shouldn't have underestimated the almighty—"

Without even waiting until the end, Seiya unsheathes his sword and makes the first move to attack the flame monster. With blinding speed, he instantly closes the distance, then slices through the beast from shoulder to hip…but it doesn't seem to have any effect. Just like how one cannot cut actual fire, there doesn't seem to be any change in the fiery monster even after being attacked.

I-is this a ghost-type monster?! Th-that would mean…!

"Seiya! Use holy water! Try rubbing it on your sword and attacking!"

But Seiya shakes his head.

"I already tried that, but it didn't work."

What...? Th-the sword already had holy water on it? When did he do that? W-wow, he really is prepared for almost anything, isn't he? Wait!

"Why didn't it work, then?! Is that not a ghost?!"

Deathmagla stifles a laugh.

"This is Dark Firus, the strongest fire-type monster in existence and, in a way, my partner—born from endless experimentation on hundreds of monsters."

"A fire-type monster?! I thought you could only create undead!"

"I can do more than create undead! My ability can re-create all types of monsters! You shouldn't just assume things, you half-wit!"

Tsk! Who are you calling a half-wit, you arrogant little...?! I mean, yeah, I assumed wrong, but so what?! Now that we know it's not an undead monster, all we have to do is change tactics!

Just as I'm about to use Scan on Dark Firus to search for its weakness...

"Do you plan on checking its status? Go ahead. Unlike *some people*, Dark Firus doesn't use cowardly abilities like Fake Out."

"...Well, I guess that means you already peeked at Seiya's status."

"I actually couldn't because his Fake Out level is so high... But that doesn't matter. Dark Firus is invincible, after all!"

Heh! He wouldn't be saying that if he could actually see Seiya's stats! I can use Goddess Power, and while I've been too afraid to look at his attributes lately, I know for a fact that he's become even stronger since his fight with Chaos Machina!

I strain my eyes and check the enemy's status. Dark Firus's attributes pop up without a fight, just like Deathmagla said they would.

DARK FIRUS

LV: 74

HP: 80,187   MP: 9,215

ATK: 31,559   DEF: 135,875   SPD: 10,741   MAG: 8,377

Resistance: Fire, Wind, Water, Lightning, Earth, Holy, Dark, Poison, Paralysis, Sleep, Curse, Instant Death, Status Ailments

Special Abilities: Null Physical (LV: MAX), Null Fire Magic (LV: MAX), Null Wind Magic (LV: MAX), Null Water Magic (LV: MAX), Null Lightning Magic (LV: MAX), Null Earth Magic (LV: MAX), Null Holy Magic (LV: MAX), Null Dark Magic (LV: MAX)

Skills: Deadly Flames

Personality: Only obeys Deathmagla

Its attack and speed easily surpass Chaos Machina's…but what surprises me most are its defense and special abilities.

"It has over one hundred thousand defense… To make matters worse, it's not only immune to physical attacks but almost all magic as well?!"

Wh-wh-what is this?! There's no way Seiya can defeat this thing! Fire magic doesn't work, and he can't use Wind Blade for obvious reasons. Even Atomic Split Slash has earth properties. Fire, wind, and earth magic won't work, and sword-based attacks won't work, either…which leaves only one thing…

"I-ice magic?! That's it?!"

"Precisely. But you can't just start using ice magic and expect it to work. There's a sequence to it."

Sensing his advantage, Deathmagla gets cocky.

"But hey, I'm a nice guy. Let me tell you how to do it. First, you need to use the skill Oscillatory Wave to create a disturbance in Dark Firus's molecular structure. Next, you need to use ice magic to change its type from fire to ice to materialize it. Only then will its Null Attack ability be removed. After that, you just need to strike Dark Firus with an attack power that surpasses its defense, and you win."

"Oh, how kind of you."

Seiya expresses his gratitude. I, on the other hand, get goose bumps all over my body. While Oscillatory Wave is a move you can learn after level 7, blunt attacks are more or less meaningless in a sword and magic world like Gaeabrande. A sword-wielding knight having a bare-knuckle blunt skill like that just doesn't make sense. Furthermore, for magic users that specialize in fire magic, it's theoretically impossible to have ice spells, since that's fire magic's weakness. *Moreover*, even if you did somehow miraculously have both of these skills, you'd still have this monster's impenetrable defense to deal with…

Deathmagla smirks while watching my face go pale.

"Do you get it? It makes no difference if I tell you how to beat Dark Firus because you'll never do it! I just wanted you to fall into despair before you die! What kind of person would learn blunt skills when they use a sword?! Regardless, it's impossible for a human to learn both fire and ice magic! They're complete opposites! Furthermore, even if you did remove its Null Attack, it still has a defense of over one hundred thousand! Your chance of defeating Dark Firus is zero!"

He cackles triumphantly.

"Hya-ha-ha-ha! Hero, I was surprised when you teleported here after cutting off my left hand! But I, Deathmagla, have already prepared for the worst!"

Then he proudly indicates the fiery monster with his chin.

"The Hero came prepared to fight undead monsters, but what awaited him was an invincible fire-type beast without any of the weaknesses possessed by the undead! I imagined every possible scenario and prepared for them all! Do you see now? This is how a true master of ingenuity prepares for battle!"

Wh-what is wrong with this guy?! He's insane! This isn't even the last battle against the last boss, but there's no way we can beat him! …N-no, even so…this Hero is overly cautious. I'm sure he prepared for this, too, and is about to do something miraculous…

I look to Seiya, entrusting him with my last sliver of hope.

"…What the hell?" Seiya murmurs.

"S-Seiya?"

"Well, this is a surprise. I can't believe it."

Wait, seriously?! Is losing really our only option?!

I am consumed by anguish, but the Hero continues staring stoically at Deathmagla.

"You prepared for every possible scenario? That's 'how a true master of ingenuity prepares for battle'? I really can't believe it. Why would you go out of your way to brag about something so obvious?"

CHAPTER 19
Even More Terrifying

Deathmagla's hooked nose twitches after hearing Seiya's slight.

"'So obvious'? What, are you saying you predicted you would be in this dilemma?"

"I expected to run into other monsters besides undead. Of course, I also expected that I would fight an enemy one day who would try to exploit the fact that I specialize in fire magic as well. That's why I made sure to devise a countermeasure."

"Oh… You devised a countermeasure…"

Deathmagla's three eyes widen in anger after parroting back Seiya's assertion.

"You half-wit! Did you not listen to what I just said?! It doesn't matter what your strategy is. You cannot defeat Dark Firus!"

Rather than Seiya, Mash is actually the first to respond to Deathmagla's enraged declaration.

"H-he's right… You can't win… No attacks work against that thing… Dark Firus is…unbeatable…!"

Right before Mash almost got his head chopped off, he showed courage that impressed even Seiya. He didn't even attempt to beg for his life. However, that bravado disappeared the moment he saw Dark Firus, and that's probably because he knows firsthand just how frightening that monster is.

*   *   *

I bite my lip.

Physical wounds can easily be healed with magic, but mental scars are another story.

This young man…will probably never rise as a warrior again…

I sense that as I wrap my arm around his quivering shoulders.

Hearing Mash's trembling voice brings a smile to Deathmagla's face.

"Finally, someone who gets it! Dark Firus is invincible! A little preparation isn't going to help you win!"

His guffaw echoes throughout the spacious torture chamber, but Seiya cuts through the laughter with his resolute tone.

"Oh, it wasn't just 'a little preparation.'"

He glares at Deathmagla in a taunting manner.

"I'm perfectly prepared."

After hearing Seiya's voice brimming with confidence, it hits me…

No… There is something—just one thing that could heal the wound in Mash's heart…!

I hold Mash tightly in my arms, then whisper in his ear as he trembles.

"Mash, do not look away. I want you to see that there is something more terrifying in this world than Deathmagla—even more terrifying than Dark Firus."

…I'm worried. I mean, realistically speaking, anxiety is the only thing I feel right now. Because even I think it's logically impossible to win against a monster like that. But Seiya, the overly cautious Hero, is talking like he always does and looking as confident as ever.

He said he's perfectly prepared! That's why…I just have to believe in him. I have to believe in the Hero I chose!

"Tsk! Let's see how tough you are after I take your head!"

Deathmagla spits this latest threat. That's when Dark Firus, currently shielding Deathmagla with its massive frame, transforms slightly. While it doesn't have eyes or a nose, the bottom half of its face—where one would expect a mouth—opens wide. The cavity is overflowing with black flames just like its body. Deathmagla looks at Mash and me, positioned directly behind Seiya, then smiles gleefully.

"Deadly Flames: Once set on fire, the flames will not go out until the target has been burned to ash! Hero, if you dodge this attack, your friends behind you will be devoured by the flames in your place! While the goddess will live, the brat will be reduced to nothing more than scorched meat!"

O-oh no! What have I done?! I should have paid more attention and gotten as far away as I could while I had the chance!

But Seiya neither acts like he blames me nor appears even the least bit worried.

"Once we get set on fire, huh? Too bad that won't be happening."

Seiya sheathes his sword before lowering his stance.

"Mn…! He's going to attack. Dark Firus—"

Before Deathmagla can even give the monster orders, Seiya is already standing directly in front of it with his right arm pulled back.

"Wh-what?! How is he that fast?!"

Deathmagla howls. After closing the distance so quickly that it looked like he teleported, Seiya swings his cocked right hand straight into Dark Firus's stomach.

A palm strike?! Wait, that's no ordinary palm strike! Not only did the hit make Dark Firus's stomach shake, but it made the air around him vibrate as well!

Th-that's… That's Oscillatory Wave!

Oscillatory Wave is a blunt body strike that is generally used to temporarily incapacitate the enemy. However, there is no change in Dark Firus's movement. Instead, the attack has a different effect on the creature by creating a disturbance in the monster's molecular structure, changing the black flames that make up its body into normal crimson ones.

Deathmagla screams.

"Y-you learned Oscillatory Wave?! Ridiculous! You're a swordsman, are you not?! Why would you learn such a useless skill?!"

"…If I was ever unable to use my sword, I would only have my fists to fight with. In light of the possibility, why wouldn't I learn unarmed combat?"

"B-but what kind of swordsman thinks like that?!"

"I never thought of myself as a swordsman. That's why I don't merely rely on my sword. After all, I expected to encounter enemies I couldn't use my sword against, and look, there's one right here. Let's not forget that blades sometimes break during battle as well. Plus, an enemy could steal my sword, or it could suddenly melt, or rust, or get eaten by insects..."

Deathmagla and I try to catch our breath while listening.

I—I guess he wouldn't be Seiya without being overly cautious, but still...! Having your sword eaten by insects is a bit of a reach... Anyway, good job, Seiya!

While Deathmagla is astonished that Seiya can use Oscillatory Wave, I'm having an epiphany.

When Seiya was pinning Cerceus and punching him in the face, he wasn't bullying him—he was practicing unarmed combat! I'm so relieved! Thank goodness!

"Y-you're every bit as cautious as the rumors said! But that all ends here! Because fire magic users can't use ice magic! ...Now go, Dark Firus! Kill him!"

I gasp in surprise, bracing myself for the flames about to shoot out of the monster's mouth. But Dark Firus raises its arm into the air and throws a punch at Seiya!

"Ha! You thought I was going to use Deadly Flames, but Dark Firus's arms are extremely hot weapons as well! They melt anything they touch!"

"S-Seiya?!"

The fist is already too close to Seiya to dodge! But that's when he throws his left fist at Dark Firus's right!

"You half-wit! Do you seriously think you can block Dark Firus's fist with your puny human hands?! Keh-keh-keh! Say good-bye to your arm!"

Dark Firus's temporarily materialized fist collides with Seiya's left hand... causing a deep rumbling that echoes so loudly, you can feel it in your stomach. I'm forced to shut my eyes in order to endure the shock waves.

...After that...I slowly open my eyes...to find their fists touching.

Seiya's hand hasn't changed, but Dark Firus's fist, then wrist, then upper arm all start to *click* and *clack* before turning blue and then finally becoming transparent!

Th-the monster is freezing?!

The phenomenon continues to its chest, then its stomach, and before long, it spreads to its entire body. Dark Firus's whole body is transforming from red to blue.

"I-ice magic?! No! No, no, no! This can't be! Ice magic and fire magic are complete opposites! Humans can't possess both!"

I don't have any idea what's going on, either. What Deathmagla is saying is true. You cannot simultaneously learn the opposite type. You cannot break the laws of magic theory.

So how did he do that?!

Only when I look hard at Seiya's arm do I realize it. He's wearing a bracer that I've never seen before! Deathmagla seems to notice this as well and raises his voice.

"W-wait! Is that—?! Is that an item that grants ice magic?!"

Ohhh! It's an ice-magic bracer! He doesn't have to use magic with that, since it fundamentally does the same thing! B-but none of the weapon or item shops we went to sold such a rare item...so where did he get it?! Wait...!

"Synthesis! Seiya, did you make that while synthesizing items?!"

Seiya nods.

"W-wow! B-but what did you combine to make such a rare item?!"

"I combined an average bracer with some ice...and then I added the usual: your hair."

"...What?"

D-don't tell me he went into my room again while I wasn't there? I—I don't know how I feel about this! But whatever! If all it takes to get out of a pinch is some of my hair, then take as much as you'd like!

"By the way, this isn't the only thing I made."

"What...?"

Like a magician, Seiya starts pulling bracers out of his pocket one after another.

"This is a lightning bracer, this one's a holy bracer, this is a dark bracer... and the list goes on. Of course, I made spares as well. And I made all these thanks to the numerous strands of hair lying around in your room."

Just how much hair do I lose every day?! Am I going bald?! Whatever.

I'll have plenty of time to think about that later. I need to focus on Dark Firus for now. The bracer seems to have frozen the monster, but it looks like it can still move. However, its flickering flames harden, materializing it. In short...

"Seiya! Your physical attacks can hurt it now!"

I'm absolutely delighted by the second miracle in a row, but in contrast to my joy, Deathmagla appears to be racked with fear.

"No! This can't be! This can't be!! You can't possibly be telling me that your attack power exceeds Dark Firus's defense as well?!"

But Seiya's answer takes me by surprise.

"Unfortunately, my attack power isn't that high yet. I probably wouldn't even be able to leave a scratch with a normal attack."

"Whaaaaat?!"

I feel like I've just fallen from heaven and dropped straight into hell. Deathmagla, on the other hand, wears an expression of relief. Ignoring both of us, the Hero continues as if he'd been talking to himself the entire time.

"But that won't be a problem now that the enemy has materialized. After all, fire magic is obviously effective against ice enemies. Unfortunately, Phoenix Drive isn't strong enough to penetrate the enemy's defense, so..."

Seiya backsteps, creating some distance between them. Sensing danger, Deathmagla screams.

"Th-this is bad! He's going to do something crazy! Dark Firus, close the distance! Keep him from attacking!"

But Seiya has already unsheathed his weapon. The silvery-white blade of the platinum sword, known for its high attack power, is wreathed in flames.

Dark Firus tries to close the distance as ordered, but...

"You're too late."

With his flaming sword drawn back, Seiya charges Dark Firus. As the two collide, a powerful shock wave shakes the room. With both arms raised, Dark Firus tries to grab Seiya...but those arms stay motionless in the air—because Seiya's sword is piercing Dark Firus's chest.

"Let the scorching flames converge into a single strike—Phoenix Thrust!"

There is a crackling sound like that of ice being shattered, and the sword goes right through Dark Firus's chest! A fissure forms where the sword entered and then spreads throughout its body.

The moment Seiya sheathes his sword, Dark Firus explodes, bursting into flames and leaving only dust behind.

"Y-you did it! We won…!"

Before I even noticed, Mash is tightly squeezing my arm.

"H-how?! What the hell is going on?! I thought he was supposed to have zero chance of winning! Why…? How? How did he beat that monster?!"

Mash is trembling but not out of fear. Color returns to his cheeks as he keeps his eyes open wide, staring at the Hero who killed the monster he once feared without sustaining a single injury.

In my excitement, I look at Deathmagla—frozen in terror—and flip him the middle finger.

"Did you see that?! That's one-in-a-billion talent right there! You like that?!"

"Th-th-this can't be…!"

Quaking, Deathmagla starts a slow retreat.

"Who's the half-wit now, half-wit? That's what you get for being so cocky that you actually told us how to win!"

Seiya fixes his messy hair while muttering:

"Well, he didn't have to even say anything. I would have figured it out soon enough."

"Yeah, I'm sure you would've! You're the perfect superhero, after all!"

Elated, I send Seiya a cheerful smile, but he turns to Deathmagla with an expression devoid of all emotion.

"After taking care of this one, I'll have to purify the entire room with everything I've got to make sure Dark Firus never comes back."

"Of course! Be my guest! Take as much time as you'd like!"

As I leave the torture chamber with Mash in tow, I can still hear the sound of Deathmagla's anguished screams.

After dampening a washcloth with cold water, I return to the room to find Mash already awake. He looks over at me from under the blanket.

"…Where am I?"

"The inn in Seimul."

A few hours ago, the moment Seiya came out of the torture chamber after finishing his so-called "purification," Mash fainted, as if all the tension had suddenly left his body. I asked Seiya to carry him as I created a gate to the spirit world. Using gates to the spirit world to travel fast within other worlds is probably against the rules. However, I was so worried about Mash that I went through the gate ready to accept any and all consequences. And just like that, we returned to the Seimul inn where Elulu awaited us.

As I try to explain that to Mash…

"Maaash!"

Elulu, who had fallen asleep near the bed, wakes up and leaps onto Mash.

"Oof!"

"Thank goodness! Thank goodness you're all right! I was so worried that you wouldn't wake up! Mash!!"

"E-Elulu?! Mash's injuries haven't completely healed yet!"

She lets go of Mash as he groans in pain.

"S-sorry, Mash. Did I hurt you?"

"N-no, it didn't hurt. I'm fine."

Mash forces a smile for a few moments until a serious expression washes away his smirk.

"It's weird… I really…don't feel any pain at all…"

He gazes at me.

"Wait… Did you heal me?"

I smile back.

"You were in terrible shape. It took over an hour to heal you."

"…I'm sorry. I owe you one," says Mash as he bashfully looks away.

That's when the door opens without a knock, revealing the ill-mannered Hero.

"Oh, Mushroom, you're awake."

But Mash doesn't even look angry. Rather, in an embarrassed manner…

"Thanks for saving me."

He thanks Seiya without looking him in the eye.

It must have taken a lot of courage for someone as strong-willed as Mash to say that, but Seiya takes no notice.

"More importantly, I hope you two are ready. It's time to go."

"S-Seiya? Come on—let's let them rest a little longer. Mash just woke up."

But Elulu and Mash look at each other, puzzled by Seiya's words.

"Um… What do you mean, 'It's time to go'?"

"I've decided to let you two carry my stuff. Now, hurry up. We're leaving."

Could he put that any more rudely?! Why couldn't he just say something like *We're going to be working together as a team from now on*? Ugh!

I'm worried about how they'll react…but Elulu is glowing with the news.

"Yay! We get to carry his stuff! I'm so happy!"

Does she even realize what she's saying?

Mash, on the other hand, wears a sullen expression, and understandably so. As if cornered, he timidly speaks up.

"It became clear to me then… You really are on a different level than us. As things are now, we'd get in the way just like you said we would. So… So…"

I inwardly sigh because I know all too well what Mash is going to say next. The trauma caused by the torture and Dark Firus must be deeply ingrained. Even if he overcame it but still decided that he didn't want to come with us, I wouldn't have any right to say anything.

However, Mash lunges out of bed, then presses his head against the floor before Seiya.

"Please make me your pupil!"

"...Huh?"

I am taken aback.

"I'll train hard so I won't get in your way! Of course, I'll carry your stuff, too! So please let me learn from you! I want to be strong like you! Please! Let me train under you!"

Wh-what the...? His mental fortitude is greater than I thought...and that makes me so happy!

Seiya looks down at Mash and bluntly states:

"I don't care what you do as long as you carry my stuff."

"O-okay! Lookin' forward to it! I mean—I look forward to working with you."

Elulu gives Seiya a carefree smile.

"Hee-hee! It's a pleasure to finally join you, Seiya!"

"E-Elulu! Don't call him by his first name! Call him 'master'!"

"...Call me whatever you want. It makes no difference to me."

Seiya seems really annoyed, but while gazing at them, I can't help but think to myself...

Well...this might not be your typical Hero's party, but the two dragonkin offspring will be joining us as planned, so I guess all's well that ends well.

Elulu tugs at the hem of my dress while innocently smiling.

"I look forward to traveling with you, too, Ristie."

"Huh? 'Ristie'? Do you mean me?"

"Do you not like the nickname...?"

"N-no, I don't really mind..."

Ha-ha-ha... I mean, I'd prefer to be called Your Majestic Godliness, but whatever.

"Oh, master! I know this may be sudden, but I have somewhere I'd like to take you!"

"Ah! Mash?! Are you talking about the Dragons' Den?!"

The Dragons' Den…? This is the first I've ever heard of it.

"Hey, Mash. What's the Dragons' Den? Is there something important there?"

…To summarize what Mash learned from the late village chief of Nakashi village:

It all began sixteen years ago. A dragon descended from the heavens and landed in Nakashi village with two infants: Mash and Elulu. The dragon said to the village chief, "These children, rich with the blood of the dragon, shall join the Hero who has received revelation from the gods and shall protect Gaeabrande from evil. When the Hero appears, go to the Dragons' Den and break the seal. The ultimate weapon, unparalleled in its ability to vanquish evil, awaits."

Exuberant, I shake Seiya by the shoulders.

"Seiya! The ultimate weapon! We have to go get it!"

But Seiya's expression is solemn as he gazes at the sword at his waist.

"But I just synthesized a platinum sword and made three spares…"

R-really? Now I feel kind of bad. But this is what adventure is all about! After working so hard and finally getting a weapon, you'll sometimes almost immediately find something even stronger!

"Let's get this adventure started! To the Dragons' Den! Mash, Elulu, lead the way!"

While these two are full of smiles and ready to go…

"Not yet."

Time stops with those few words.

"I have somewhere I have to go first."

"S-Seiya… Don't tell me you're going to—"

"Yes, to the spirit world. I can't afford to ignore my training."

Crushed, I drop my head.

Every time… We go on a little adventure, and then we're right back in the spirit world… The Summoning Chamber's starting to feel like home…

"We're going to the Dragons' Den next, right? I have to make sure I'm prepared to fight dragons."

Mash and Elulu turn pale, as one would expect.

"M-master, please don't! Are you trying to make us go extinct or something?!"

"Y-yeah! There's no such thing as a bad dragon! Probably."

"We won't know until we go. At any rate, I'm going to the spirit world, and you're coming with me. Rista, it wouldn't be a problem if we brought them, right?"

"Yeah… I guess…"

I have mixed feelings about all this but give my approval.

I've decided not to say anything, since he has proven that training in the unified spirit world is actually working. If Seiya did what I, someone who has summoned only a few Heroes, suggested and fought monsters to level up, then he probably would have already been killed. Gaeabrande is an S-ranked world. What was common sense in past worlds isn't common sense here. The best thing to do is to leave everything in Seiya's hands.

I cast a spell and create the gate. Following Seiya, Mash and Elulu almost skip through as if they were going on vacation.

After arriving in the unified spirit world, Seiya immediately asks where Cerceus is. Given it's around noon at the moment and he usually takes his lunch breaks in the dining hall, we decide to head straight there.

Elulu's eyes dart about for the entirety of the walk through the sanctuary.

"Hey, Ristie! This is where all the gods and goddesses live, right?!"

"Yep."

Mash gets an eyeful as well.

"This sanctuary is amazing. Not only is it huge, but the decorations, the paintings—everything I see is art… Not like I know much about that, though."

"Whoa! Look at the beautiful flowers in that vase! I've never seen anything like them! Hey, Ristie! Can I go have a look?!"

"Elulu, hold up! Look at that guy over there! He's got a halo floating over his head! Is he an angel?!"

Seeing Elulu and Mash so excited fills me with warmth. I can't blame them. Most people would react this way during their first time in the spirit world…unlike some who just lock themselves away for a few days in a white room and work out.

The abnormal Hero grabs Elulu by the back of the neck like a cat, stopping her in the middle of her exploration.

"You can do that later. I want to start training."

"Mn…! But there's so much more I want to see!"

"S-Seiya, I don't mind going to see Cerceus, but I don't think he's going to spar with you anymore."

"I don't care about that. I need him for something else."

Then why are you…?

Confused, I continue walking until we arrive at the dining hall. I survey the vast room, but Cerceus is nowhere in sight. We give up and decide to check somewhere else, but right before leaving the hall, I randomly make eye contact with a familiar face in the kitchen at the other end.

I hear a faint "eep!" coming from the kitchen, then see a man dressed in an apron try to crouch down and hide.

…There's no mistaking who that is.

"Cerceus?!"

I force my way into the kitchen…and can't believe my eyes.

The well-built, muscular Divine Blade is wearing a floral-print apron with a silver bowl of meringue in hand.

"…What are you doing?"

Seiya glares at Cerceus, causing the latter's back to bolt up stock straight.

"S-S-Sir Seiya! How are you doing today?!"

Blech… There's nothing godlike about him anymore… I mean, he's talking to Seiya like the Hero is his superior… And there's just something about that beard with that apron… They don't make sense together at all…

Cerceus's eyes wander as he speaks.

"So, uh… As you know…I was thinking about quitting swordsmanship. I mean, it's dangerous, you know? Like, you bleed when you get cut and it hurts and, like…"

What the—?! That wasn't a joke?! The Divine Blade is seriously giving up the blade?! Just how traumatic was his training with Seiya?!

Cerceus bashfully shows us the bowl full of meringue.

"S-so lately, I've been learning how to cook. See? …Oh yeah! I just baked a cake. Would you like to try a piece?"

He retrieves a plate with a strawberry shortcake and shows it to Seiya. It's

visually impressive to the point that it's hard to believe this gorilla of a man made it. However, the moment Seiya lays eyes on it...

"Disgusting. Get that away from me."

"But you didn't even try it!" yells Cerceus.

I can't blame him. Anyone would react that way if someone said their food was disgusting without trying it.

"I worked so hard to make this...!"

That's when the poor guy notices a redheaded girl who looks like she might just happen to like sweets. He smiles.

"What about you? Would you like to try some?"

He holds out a fork and knife to Elulu, but she shakes her head.

"Hmm... No thanks. I mean, I bet it's full of muscles or something..."

"...?! It doesn't have any muscles in it! Wait! How would you even put muscles in a cake?!"

Seiya stares at the pitiful man holding the unwanted cake.

"Listen, Cerceus. I'm not saying you can't have a hobby. But that's not your calling, and you need to focus on that before anything else."

"M-my calling...?"

"I'm referring to this, of course."

Seiya unsheathes his platinum sword, revealing the radiant blade.

"Noooooo! I don't wanna spar anymooooooore!!" Cerceus screams. It's a howl that even has Mash questioning the god's mental stability.

"Don't worry. I'm not going to be the one training with you. He is."

Mash is just as surprised as Cerceus.

"Huh? Y-you're not going to be the one training me?"

"You're not ready for me. He should be around your level, though."

"Wow, Seiya. You're really looking out for Mash."

"Well, I can't let the errand boy carrying my stuff be weak. It would defeat the purpose of having him if a monster simply stole everything from him."

Cerceus glances at Mash a few times, a boy only half his size.

"I-is he your disciple? Uh... Would you mind if I used Scan on you for a moment?"

"Be my guest."

After timidly casting Scan, Cerceus stares at him for a while with a dubious glare.

"Hmm? You're not using Fake Out, right?"

"No... Why?"

Suddenly, Cerceus tears off his floral-print apron.

"All right! Let's do this! I've gotta warn ya, though. Training with me is gonna be tough! I hope you're ready! Gwa-ha-ha-ha!"

"Wh-what is wrong with this geezer?! His personality is all over the place!"

Mash is right. Cerceus is... I don't even know what to say! He started acting all tough the moment he discovered that Mash was weaker than him! These types of guys are the worst!

With a new spring in his step, Cerceus escorts Mash out of the kitchen. After that, Seiya turns his gaze to Elulu.

"All right, you're up next."

"Huh?! M-m-me too?!"

Elulu's astonished voice resonates throughout the kitchen.

CHAPTER 21
God of War

"If I'm remembering correctly, this little girl specializes in fire magic like me."

Paying no heed to Elulu's fidgeting, Seiya looks at me.

"Rista, are there any gods in the spirit world who specialize in fire magic?"

"Well, there's the Goddess of Fire... She might be able to help us."

"Good. Take us to her."

"Sure."

As I try to start walking, Elulu grabs the hem of my dress and looks up at me with eyes drowning in worry.

"What's wrong, Elulu?"

"Ristie... Is the fire god nice like you?"

She probably imagined some sort of angry, unforgiving deity when she heard that she was a fire god. I send her a smile.

"You've got nothing to worry about! Unlike Cerceus, Hestiaca is a wonderful, loving goddess!"

"R-really?! Thank goodness!"

Elulu's usual cheerful smile returns to her lips.

After that, I begin guiding them to the reflecting pond past the courtyard. With breathtakingly clear water, the pond is about the size of a small lake, despite being within the sanctuary's premises. Hestiaca often practices her fire magic there, but there's no sign of her yet.

Hopeful, I continue heading toward the pond…until I see birds made out of fire magic gliding through the air off in the distance. There's no doubt about it. Hestiaca's here.

As expected, I find Hestiaca near the crystal clear pond with a massive firebird on her arm. As one might expect from the Goddess of Fire, she seems to have an attachment to the color red, as evidenced by her crimson dress. Coupled with her long, wavy red hair, one might mistakenly think she was completely red at first glance.

Before I can greet her, she notices me.

"Ristarte, it's been quite a while."

"Hestiaca! I'm sorry I'm so bad at keeping in touch!"

She speaks with a clear voice, then looks over at Seiya and Elulu.

"Oh, who do we have here? Are these your Heroes, Rista?"

"Yes! That's actually why we're here."

I ask if she would be willing to teach Elulu fire magic.

"It is the duty of all the deities in the spirit world to support the humans trying to save their homes. I would be more than happy to help."

Hestiaca agrees to cooperate without a moment's hesitation.

Elulu bows deeply.

"I-I'm E-Elulu! Nice to meet you!"

Hestiaca gently rubs Elulu's head, but Elulu's stone stiff due to her nerves.

"What beautiful red hair you have. Hee-hee… I suppose that makes us twins, don't you think? Anyway, there's no reason to be so nervous. I won't bite."

"O-okay!"

"Now then, shall we begin? Show me your fire magic…"

As Seiya and I start walking away from the pond, we watch Elulu cast Fire Arrow into the sky. Elulu is in good hands. Mash, on the other hand, I'm worried about. I'll have to go check up on him later.

Seiya stretches his back while strolling down the path we came from.

"All right, then. Time to find my new training partner."

I regard him disdainfully. Seiya is acting like he has just been released from all obligations.

He reminds me of a deadbeat parent who drops their noisy kids off at a neighbor's house and never comes home...but maybe I'm thinking too much about it.

Hmm... At any rate, we need to find a god stronger than Cerceus. The unified spirit world is a big place, so I'm sure there are plenty if you look for them, but I can't think of anyone off the top of my head. Returning to the sanctuary and asking Aria is probably my best bet...

Thanks to my daydreaming, I don't even notice the goddess right in front of me until we bump shoulders.

"Huh? Ah! I-I'm so sorry!"

I immediately apologize, but...

"Tch! Watch where you're goin', bitch!" she yells menacingly before grabbing my lapel.

"Eek!"

Her intimidating voice and appearance make my heart race. She has a beautiful but boyish visage with short silver hair. The only clothes she's wearing (if you can even call them clothes) are the chains wrapped around her chest and lower body. Valkyrie, the Goddess of Destruction, brings her face closer to mine.

"Ristarte, you good-for-nothing, third-rate goddess! You got a death wish? Is that it?"

"I-I-I'm so sorry! Please forgive me, Valkyrie!"

I apologize profusely. After looking me up and down with a "hmph," she smirks.

"By the way, Ristarte, I heard they gave you an S-ranked world. So? How's it going?"

"Oh, uh... Well...I'm working really hard on it at the moment—"

"Pfft! A third-rate goddess like you doesn't stand a chance!"

"Ha-ha... O-oh, you don't say."

I try to put on a smile, but out of nowhere, my chest suddenly starts feeling weird.

"Huh...?"

Only when I glance down do I realize that Valkyrie is groping my breasts!

"H-hey?! Valkyrie?!"

"Ha-ha-ha! At least you've got some nice tits on ya! They're even bigger than mine and perfect for squeezin'!"

"P-p-please stop!"

But she doesn't stop. She continues excessively massaging my breasts.

U-unf! If she keeps touching me like this…!

"S-stop! Ah…! Ah…! Mm… P-please…stop…!"

I beg with tears in my eyes until Valkyrie finally relents.

"All right, consider us even now. I'll let ya off the hook this time, but it better not happen again, Ristarte!"

Valkyrie cackles as she walks away.

Ugh! This is sexual harassment! Goddess of Destruction? More like Goddess of Perverts! How is such a depraved goddess even allowed to live in the spirit world?!

My dress's lapels are wrinkled, and I'm on the verge of tears…which is when I notice Seiya staring at me pityingly.

"Are you being bullied in the spirit world?"

"No! Valkyrie acts like that with everyone!"

I mean, I can't deny that people look down on me because I'm new and a low-ranking goddess! That still doesn't mean I'm being bullied, though… Well, at least, that's what I like to think!

"At any rate, could you sense that exhibitionist's tremendous power?"

"Exhibitionist…? Wait. Seiya, you could tell? That was the Goddess of Destruction, Valkyrie—the strongest goddess in the unified spirit world. Rankwise, she's second only to Ishtar, and she possesses a lot of authority. It's too bad her personality sucks. Oh, and Seiya? Don't get any ideas. Training with her is out of the question, okay? She's a monster. Trust me. She wouldn't even hesitate to dispose of gods and goddesses who defy her. And humans? Forget it. She'd kill you on the spot for disrespecting her."

I pause, then look up from adjusting my lapels to discover Seiya isn't even there.

…Huh…?

…Lo and behold, Seiya is already a few dozen meters ahead talking to Valkyrie.

"Hey, exhibitionist, spar with me."

Ahhhhhh! Has he lost his mind?!

"Who are you calling an exhibitionist?"

She glares at Seiya as if he just killed her parents.

"Just 'cause you were summoned to be a Hero doesn't mean the rest of us deities have to like you, ya little shit. Disrespect me again, and I'll split ya in half."

"Oh yeah? Try it, then."

I frantically lunge in between them.

"S-stopppppp! S-Seiya!! Apologize! Apologize to her this instant!"

I don't care how strong Seiya is! He wouldn't stand a chance! She's the strongest goddess in the entire unified spirit world, and she's nowhere near as understanding as Ishtar! If he pisses her off, she will literally kill him!

Valkyrie's godly spirit radiates from her body as she glares at Seiya.

"Sorry, Ristarte. It's too late to apologize! This guy's dead!"

"W-wait…!"

Ahhh!! We're never going to save Gaeabrande if you do that! S-somebody help!!

That's when…

"Please stop!"

I hear a familiar voice and immediately see Aria panting while rushing this way.

"Valkyrie! Please lay down your weapon!"

"No can do. This human's insolence is worth a thousand deaths."

"But he is an extraordinary Hero summoned to save an S-ranked world! I beg of you. Please forgive him! Do it for me!"

Valkyrie ponders to herself for a few moments.

"Well, I guess I could forgive him if you're the one asking, Aria."

Then she leans in toward Aria.

"But in return, you have to let me feel those massive tits next time."

"O-okay…"

Aria faintly blushes. Valkyrie laughs as she leaves. As I let out a deep sigh of relief, Aria gives Seiya a piece of her mind.

"That was reckless, Seiya! You can't speak to Valkyrie that way! What do you think would have happened if I hadn't been walking by? I can't believe you!"

Huh? Strange… A-Aria's kind of talking like me… She's really letting him have it.

But Seiya doesn't even blink.

"You and Rista got too worked up. That goddess was just baiting us so she could enjoy our reactions. The fact that I couldn't sense any bloodlust proves that."

Aria and I blankly stare at each other.

"R-really? Well…you seem sure of it, Seiya, so I'm not going to doubt you…"

There's something different about the way Aria is talking today. Seiya seems to have noticed as well.

"Anyway, weren't you a lot more reserved when we first met? Since when did you start caring what I did?"

Aria places a hand on her mouth in surprise.

"I-I'm terribly sorry about that."

After clearing her throat, Aria tries to change the subject.

"A-anyway, you're looking for a training partner to take Cerceus's place, right? I know just the person. Follow me."

Aria ends up bringing us to the sanctuary's basement. After descending the long stone staircase, we walk down a narrow path that's dimly lit by the occasional wall torch.

I never knew a place like this existed within the sanctuary…

I am once again in awe of the vastness of this place. Soon enough, we reach the end of the path, and Aria stops in front of a door. It looks like we've reached our destination.

The wooden door creaks as Aria opens it. A little girl sits with her legs crossed while sharpening a sword in the bleak, prisonlike stone room. Aria introduces us inside the dimly lit chamber.

"This is the goddess Adenela. She knows even more about martial arts than Cerceus."

The spirit world sure is a big place, including the sanctuary. There are over ten thousand gods and goddesses living here, so there are many deities I haven't even met yet—Adenela, the Goddess of War, being one of them.

"Adenela, would you be able to train with this Hero?"

Adenela turns her vacant gaze to Seiya and me, revealing the dark circles under her eyes.

"Tr-tr-train? W-with a human? Heh-heh-heh-heh…"

Enunciating poorly, she speaks with a loose mouth. Her unkempt hair is long and scraggly, and she wears ragged, prisoner-like clothing. To tell the truth, Adenela doesn't look anything like a goddess. And to be completely honest, she kind of weirds me out.

"Ew. This goddess is seriously creeping me out. Ugh, disgusting."

Ah?! Why did he just say what I was thinking?! I mean, it's the truth, but still…! That's the kind of thing you're supposed to keep to yourself!

I fear this may turn into another heated situation like with Valkyrie, but…

"Heh-heh-heh-heh! Su-sure, Aria. I l-like t-t-teaching, after all. S-so let's get started."

As soon as Adenela says this, she vanishes. I shudder. How is she already behind Seiya?! As I gape in blank amazement, Adenela snickers while I stare at Seiya.

"Y-you were able to k-keep your eyes on me, huh? It appears you have potential, s-seeing as how Aria recommended you. M-maybe you'll be able to learn my special move—Eternal Sword. N-nobody has ever been able to l-learn it before. I-it exceeds humans' range of movement b-because of its lightning speed, s-so I don't blame anyone for not being able to learn it. Th-their bodies would apparently b-break down first. Heh-heh-heh…"

Ack… She's almost as bad as Valkyrie. What's Seiya going to do? It appears Aria introducing us to her, but he should really think about it bef—

"Okay. Let's do this."

"Seiya?!"

Why isn't he more cautious at times like this?! He was reckless earlier with Valkyrie, and now this! Unbelievable!

"Teach me that Unlimited Boredom move of yours."

"Heh-heh… I-it's called Eternal Sword."

"Whatever. Follow me. We're going to the Summoning Chamber."

"Heh-heh-heh. Y-you've got guts. Let's go…"

Seiya takes Adenela and leaves. Left behind, I worriedly turn to Aria.

"A-are they going to be all right?"

"Adenela is very strong, and I am certain Seiya will be able to learn her special move."

It's a relief to hear that. I bow.

"Aria, thank you so much for always helping me."

"Don't worry. It's nothing, really. I want to do everything I can to help. It's the very least I can do to…"

"…Aria?"

She falls silent with a serious look on her face.

"Oh, never mind. Forget I said anything."

Then her usual gentle smile returns to her lips.

CHAPTER 22
Madness

A day goes by. When I head over to the courtyard, I see Mash and Cerceus training together with wooden swords. With sweat dropping off his forehead, Mash gallantly rushes in to strike, but Cerceus easily parries, knocking the sword away. Mash groans.

…Wow, Cerceus! I'm impressed! You were pretending to be seaweed only a few days ago, but it turns out you're not a complete idiot!

Seeing him like this has actually raised my opinion of him, even if only slightly.

"All right, let's take a break."

"Nah, I'm gonna keep going for a little while longer. You can go take a break by yourself, though, old man."

"Okay, but don't hurt yourself, kid."

Leaving Mash to practice his swordsmanship by himself, Cerceus walks over to me.

"Rista, he's a tough kid, that Mash. Brave, too. And he's only going to get tougher."

He smirks, brimming with confidence, while wiping the sweat off with a rag.

"I'm pretty tough myself. Fighting that super-berserker made me think I was weak, but after training with Mash, I figured out that Seiya was just the exception. I'm actually rather strong."

"O-oh, wonderful."

I mean, I don't really care, but…I'm glad those two are getting along. I want to say hello to Mash, but as I'd rather not disturb his training, I retire from the courtyard.

Elulu is training with Hestiaca, so she's in good hands. It's Seiya I'm concerned about. Be that as it may, Seiya hates it when people come into the Summoning Chamber while he's training, so my chances of checking in on his training are slim. In spite of that, I make Seiya some lunch and head toward the Summoning Chamber when I notice Adenela sitting in the darkness between two walls. Her legs are crossed, and she's sharpening a sword.

"Adenela…? What happened to training?"

"I-I'm taking a break. Seiya is still t-training inside, though."

Ha-ha… They're kind of similar. Neither of them really takes breaks.

"So how's Seiya doing?"

"H-he's a unique one. Never seen a Hero like him. I'm a l-little surprised. And…"

"And…?"

"And… Heh-heh-heh-heh-heh-heh-heh-heh-heh-heh-heh-heh-heh."

"Hey…! What's wrong with you?! You're laughing like you just lost your mind!"

"I-it's nothing. I was just th-thinking about how f-fun it is training with Seiya."

That was her laughing because she remembered something nice?! Should I be worried about her?!

Just when I start getting concerned for Seiya, the doors to the Summoning Chamber open. He walks out of the room, appearing no different than usual.

"Adenela, you done yet with your break? I want to get back to training."

"I-I'll be right there…"

Adenela cheerfully skips her way through the door, and it immediately closes behind her.

"…Oh."

That's when I realize that I forgot to give Seiya his lunch, so I end up sliding it under the door like always.

But after seeing Seiya, it looks like everything's going according to plan, so I guess there's nothing I really need to worry about...

Day two of training. Noon.

Feeling hungry, I make my way to the dining hall where I find two familiar faces sitting at a corner table together.

Well, if it isn't Seiya and Mash.

Mash is nibbling a bit of bread, while Seiya drinks some water out of a cup.

"Whoa! I wasn't expecting to run into you here, Seiya!"

Seiya looks annoyed, then says, "He suddenly showed up at the Summoning Chamber and begged me to meet him during the lunch break, so here I am."

"Wait. Mash, really?"

"I—I just thought it would be nice to spend lunch with Master Seiya..."

Mash has really started to idolize Seiya. I understand how he feels, though. Seiya did save his life, after all.

"And he taught me how to mentally prepare myself for battle!"

"Oh really?! What's the secret?"

The moment I sit across from Seiya, he gets out of his seat.

"I should be getting back. Adenela's waiting."

What the...? What a jerk. It wouldn't hurt to just chat every once in a while...

I talk over Mash, who's thanking Seiya as he walks away.

"Hey, Seiya! Don't forget we're going to Gaeabrande tomorrow!"

Tomorrow will only be the third day of training, so I doubt Seiya's going to be able to learn her special move by then. But I'm kind of worried about staying here too long and being summoned by Ishtar again. Temporarily returning to Gaeabrande tomorrow is what I decided after hours of worrying.

"I'm really sorry about this. I'm just concerned about Gaeabrande, you know? But I don't mind if you want to come back to train again after going to the Dragons' Den and getting that really powerful weapon."

But Seiya doesn't even look back as he says:

"That's fine. I'll be done by tomorrow."

"You'll be...done? Seiya...?"

The Hero briskly walks off alone.

Th-there is no way he's going to learn that move with only one day left...

With Seiya gone, only Mash and I remain. I approach him while he picks at his bread.

"Hey, about that thing you mentioned a second ago. How did Seiya tell you to mentally prepare for battle?"

His eyes suddenly light up.

"Oh man. The way he thinks blows me away! Listen to this, Rista. Like, for example, when you're walking in a field, you want to make sure you're always keeping an eye out for monsters. First, look right, then left, then up, down, behind you, and then right again. Then you continue doing that until you reach your destination!"

"Uh... Would you ever even make it to your destination like that? And wouldn't you get kind of dizzy or nauseous?"

"I dunno. I mean, it might take a little longer to get where you're going, but it's safe. Anyway, what impressed me the most was when he said, *'Doubt everything you see. Everyone is the enemy, even your family.'* Is that cool or what?!"

What in the...? Does he want Mash to be jumping at shadows because he's so scared?

But Mash cheerfully smirks.

"But you know what, Rista? I haven't even told you the coolest part. After that, he looked at me and said, *'Listen, Mash. I don't trust you, either.'* What a badass thing to say!"

"How did that not piss you off?!"

"Why would that make me angry?"

"Well...if you're fine with it, then that's all that matters."

I let out a small sigh while watching Mash happily eat his bread.

And just like that, Seiya's church of caution gains a new member...

Bringing Seiya his dinner that night, I coincidentally run into Adenela as she's exiting the Summoning Chamber.

"Oh! Adenela, how's…the…?"

I stop myself from asking her how the training's going because I'm taken aback by how she's dressed. Her ragged clothes are now gone, and she's wearing a pure-white dress. Her unkempt hair is now beautifully brushed, and her dead-fishlike eyes are now glittering and full of life. She's adorable.

"Wh-wh-what happened to you?! You look like a new person!"

She blushes.

"I—I couldn't meet Seiya in the clothes I had before. Th-that'd be so embarrassing…"

Ew?! H-has she fallen for Seiya or something?! Aria was acting weird around him, too… What a playboy! I knew he was a goddessizer! He doesn't have a Seduce Goddess ability, does he?!

I shake Adenela's shoulders as she stares off into space, no doubt thinking about Seiya.

"Adenela! Pull yourself together!"

"Huh…? Oh."

"A-anyway, we'll have to postpone learning that special move of yours, since we're going back to Gaeabrande tomorrow."

"Eternal Sword? S-Seiya can already use that."

"What…? Whaaaaaat?! No way! But I thought you said nobody's ever been able to learn it?! What happened to it exceeding the limits of human movement?!"

"Yes, I said that. B-but Seiya was able to do it. He's a ge-genius. He's quick to grasp new concepts. H-he's the only human who's ever earned my trust. A-and…"

Adenela aimlessly gazes up at the ceiling. Drool drips slovenly from her gaping mouth.

"Heh-heh-heh-heh-heh… He's truly…heh-heh-heh…s-so amazing…!"

Urgh! I've got a really bad feeling about this!

Seeing her reaction tells me I made the right decision to return to Gaeabrande tomorrow.

It's the third day since training started. Though originally planning to leave a little after noon, I advanced the schedule and decided to depart

the unified spirit world in the morning. I made sure to tell everyone beforehand, so when I go to the courtyard, I find Mash already thanking Cerceus.

"Thank you so much, old man! I feel like I've gotten a lot stronger thanks to you!"

"I should be the one thanking you! You saved me from that nightmare!"

They exchange a manly handshake.

I have no words, but hey, as long as they're having fun.

I suddenly find my curiosity getting the best of me, so I look at Mash and use Scan.

MASH

LV: 16

HP: 1,381   MP: 0

ATK: 921   DEF: 877   SPD: 790   MAG: 0   GRW: 47

Resistance: Fire, Ice, Poison

Special Abilities: ATK Boost (LV: 5)

Skills: Dragon Thrust, Dragon Slash

Personality: Brave

…What?! He's leveled up a ton! He even has over 1,000 HP now! He won't be having problems against the average monster from here on out! Mash really has potential. Or is Cerceus just a really good teacher?

After bowing to Cerceus, I take Mash and head over to the reflective pond where Elulu and Hestiaca are.

When we arrive, I find Elulu squatting by the pond by herself. I haven't seen her since the first day of training when I told her the plan.

Mash cheerfully greets her.

"Yo, Elulu!"

"Ah… Mash."

"Good morning, Elulu! Ready to go?"

"Y-yep!"

Elulu looks at Mash and me, then smiles like always. I feel like there's something a little awkward about her smile, though.

I secretly use Scan on her.

ELULU

LV: 8

HP: 384   **MP: 220**

ATK: 101   **DEF: 172**   **SPD: 88**   **MAG: 196**   **GRW: 38**

Resistance: Fire, Water, Lightning

Special Abilities: Fire Magic (LV: 4)

Skills: Fire Arrow

Personality: Optimist

Uh… What? Did she gain only one level…?

As I stare at her status, I feel somebody suddenly tap me on the shoulder. I turn around to find Hestiaca, and she whispers into my ear.

"Rista, can I have a word with you?"

"Su-sure."

We head to a spot a short distance away from the pond so we can be alone. Then Hestiaca lets out a sigh while confiding:

"I'm going to be honest about Elulu. She's terrible at fire magic."

"What?! S-seriously?!"

"You used Scan on her, right? You saw. She barely leveled up at all."

With a solemn expression, she continues.

"At first, I thought I was just a bad teacher, but after three days, it became clear to me. Fire magic simply isn't for her. No question about it."

The shocking truth pains my heart. Hestiaca looks pained to admit it as well.

"Elulu is a good girl. She practiced extremely hard, too. But as you know, the talents you're born with greatly affect magic. It's hard for me to say this, but she doesn't have *it*. She's better off giving up on fire magic and cutting her losses while she's ahead. This is for her own good. At any rate, I don't know what it could be, but maybe there's a different type of magic that would be a better fit for her."

After returning to the pond alone, Elulu rushes over to me with a remorseful gaze.

"Ristie… I'm so sorry."

"Huh? Wh-what's wrong, Elulu?"

"I didn't improve much, did I? Right? That's what you were just talking with Hestiaca about, right?"

After seeing the tears well up in her eyes, I just can't tell her the truth. In fact…

"Wh-what are you talking about, Elulu?! Yes, you're a slow starter, but you're doing just fine! You don't have to rush things! Hestiaca told me that, too!"

I try to encourage her, and immediately, she smiles back at me adorably.

"Really?! Okay! I'll keep at it, then! I've tried so many types of magic, but fire magic is the only one I've ever been good at, so I'm gonna work really hard on it!"

"Y-yeah! That's the spirit, Elulu!"

Ugh… I'm the worst… I'm a terrible goddess…

I may hate myself right now, but it's still better than telling her the truth. If I'm going to tell her the coldhearted truth, it'll have to be at the right moment. I have no idea what the "right moment" even is, though.

At any rate, I still can't believe this happened. I mean, I thought Hestiaca and Elulu were going to be fine, but…I guess sometimes things don't turn out the way you want them to.

Nevertheless, I take Mash and Elulu with me and head to the Summoning Chamber.

When we arrive, we find Seiya leaning against a wall by the door.

"Seiya, are you ready to go?"

"Yeah. But Adenela said she wanted to give me something, so…"

Sh-she wanted to give you something? I can't imagine what.

"She did teach me a lot, so I'm waiting for her out of obligation. She is really taking her time, though. If she isn't back here within the next minute, we're leaving."

But just as he finishes that sentence, Adenela comes jogging over. It goes without saying that she's well-dressed again, but it looks like she also put on some makeup.

She runs and jumps right into Seiya's arms.

"What the…?! Adenela?! What are you doing?!"

As I watch in a stupor, she looks up at Seiya with puppy dog eyes and speaks to him in an affectionate, needy voice.

"Seiya… T-take me with you o-on your journey…"

"Adenela?! *I'm* his goddess, you know!"

"Th-then let me c-come as one of the Hero's party m-members…"

"But you're a goddess! You can't do that!"

"I-I'll quit b-being a goddess, then! I don't ever w-wanna be away from Seiya!"

Her surprising confession of love almost makes me faint. Somehow keeping myself together, I look at Seiya to see how he'll react. However, he doesn't say anything and appears as indifferent as always. Adenela then takes out a small package to hand to him.

"I made th-this for you! It's a c-cake! It t-took me five hours to make, but I want you t-to have it…!"

A homemade cake?! Wait! If he takes that cake, does that mean he accepts her love?! S-Seiya, don't! Hold up… Cake…?

The events from three days ago when Seiya harshly criticized Cerceus's cake flash across the back of my mind.

H-he wouldn't say that to a lady, right?! Seiya, you don't need to accept the cake, but…but you better not say anything rude!

But Seiya replies without missing a beat.

"Disgusting. Get that away from me."

He said it agaaaaaaain! He called the cake "disgusting" without even tasting it agaaaaaaain!

I look back at Adenela, and as expected, she's gone white as snow.

But Seiya doesn't stop there. He immediately starts pouring salt into the wound.

"I appreciate you training me these past few days. However, that's all our relationship will ever be. I have no interest in you, and I don't want your cake. Farewell."

Then Seiya swiftly turns on his heel before walking straight down the marble hallway, not looking back for a second. Mash and Elulu follow closely behind.

"Yeah… I get it… I'm u-unwanted…heh-heh-heh-heh…just like this cake…heh-heh-heh-heh-heh-heh-heh-heh-heh-heh-heh-heh."

"A-Adenela?! …Ahhh!"

The instant I look at her, I reflexively let out a scream.

Tears of blood run down Adenela's cheeks…

I dash after Seiya and scold him when I finally catch up.

"Seiya! You should feel bad for what you did to Adenela!"

"Feel bad for what? She helped me train to save Gaeabrande. What's so bad about that?"

"I'm talking about what you did after that! You didn't have to be so rude! Think about how she must have felt! You made her cry, you know! *Tears of blood!*"

"That's not my problem. More importantly, create the gate, Rista. And, you two—hold my stuff."

Seiya hands them rucksacks full of items.

Sigh… What a jerk. He may have told the truth, but how he said it was just awful… If he ever finds out that Elulu doesn't have a gift for magic, I don't even want to imagine what he'll say.

As soon as I create a gate to Gaeabrande, I hear screams coming from outside the sanctuary.

"Ahhh!! Adenela is beating the statue in the courtyard with her sword!"

"A-Adenela! Please stop!"

"I beg of you! Calm your anger! Somebody stop her!"

"Easier said than done! Do you know how strong she—? Gwaaah?!"

The courtyard is thrown into an uproar, but Seiya acts as if it has nothing to do with him. He combs back his glossy black hair, then says:

*   *   *

"I'm perfectly prepared."

Nobody asked! What are you going to do about the trouble you caused?! Ugh! Unbelievable! This better not turn into my problem!

...I swiftly follow Seiya through the gate, leaving the unified spirit world like a fugitive.

CHAPTER 23
Izale Village

From what Mash heard from his village chief, the Dragons' Den is said to be far east of Krain Castle. The village chief also said that dragonkin will naturally be able to sense the cave's location when they are nearby.

Anyway, I made the gate take us to the forest around Krain Castle, which Ishtar told me about when we were saving Mash. Seiya starts complaining as soon as everyone exits the gate.

"You should have had us appear in front of an item shop somewhere."

"An item shop…? Wh-why?"

"We're going to a cave, right? Not only are we going to need torches, but we need to prepare food, water, and other necessities as well."

Elulu curiously looks up at Seiya.

"B-but, Seiya, I don't think there are any monsters in this cave. I heard it was a holy place used to seal the ultimate weapon."

"Don't be naive. Who knows what could be there? We need to prepare."

"W-well, I'm sure we'll run into a town or village along the way. Anyway, we should probably get going."

I try to appease the cautious Hero as we walk. However, the second we make it out of the forest, Seiya grouchily complains:

"Why are we walking all the way there? You should have just asked Ishtar to take us to a safe town near the Dragons' Den."

"W-we can't do that! No shortcuts allowed! We have to start from a point near where we left off!"

I mean, Heroes don't normally even get to go back and forth between the human world and the spirit world like Seiya does constantly!

"It doesn't make sense to waste time like that when we're supposed to be saving the world."

"Well, there's nothing we can do about it! I told you already. By law, we are prohibited to excessively help humans on their quests! Besides, walking like this can be fun every once in a while! Right, Mash?"

I glance over at Mash, and he firmly nods back.

"Yeah! I can't wait to fight a monster! I want to see how strong I've gotten from training with Cerceus!"

"Right?!"

While we hit it off, Seiya heaves a small sigh and begins power walking, as if he's resigned himself to traveling to the Dragons' Den on foot.

We end up following Seiya across the plains for a good twenty minutes.

Hearing panting from behind, I turn around to see Elulu struggling. When I approach her to hold the bag she's carrying, I see a small fire in between her hands, to my surprise.

"Huh? What are you doing, Elulu?"

"Oh, um... Hestiaca taught me this. She said I could practice magic like this even while walking. It's really exhausting, though."

"So that's why you were breathing so heavily."

"Yep! I really wanna make sure I can help Seiya and Mash if a monster ever attacks!"

Seiya apparently hears Elulu's courageous comment and turns.

"You don't need to do that. All you need to worry about is carrying my stuff."

"O-oh yeah! Ha-ha...ha..."

She's smiling, but I can tell the light in her eyes just dimmed a little.

"Seiya!!"

I get ready to give Seiya an earful until he murmurs, "Besides, no monsters are going to show up."

Now that I think about it, we've been walking for a long time now, but I haven't seen a single monster. This isn't supposed to be that safe of an area, either. So what's going on?

Before long, I notice something squirming on the horizon. With better eyesight than humans, I can see the face of a vile-looking pig monster walking our way on two legs.

"Mash! Do you see that? Is that an orc?"

"Oh, you're right! It is an orc! Heh. This should make for a good warm-up!"

After drawing his sword, Mash starts rushing toward the orc in the distance…until a colossal firebird suddenly comes raining down from the skies. It's even bigger than the ones Hestiaca made at the reflective pond. It instantly swoops down and slams into the orc, engulfing it in flames and causing it to instantly collapse. Elulu latches onto my arm.

"Wh-what kind of monster was that?!"

"Did that thing just blow itself up along with the orc?!"

Monsters fighting each other?! Wait. W-was that even a monster?! If not, then that would mean…

"Everyone, watch out! There's probably a sorcerer nearby!"

Elulu and Mash immediately take a defensive position. As a tense air reigns over the three of us, Seiya speaks in a composed manner.

"Relax. I made it."

"""Huh?"""

Overcome with surprise, the three of us stare at Seiya.

"Automatic Phoenix. It can detect monsters' evil auras within a fifty-meter radius and will automatically attack the target with a fire-based attack."

Th-that was Seiya's magic?! Long-range fire magic…? I mean, I'm amazed, but…

"W-wow, that was incredible, master! But let me handle the next one!"

That's when Elulu screams.

"Ah! Mash! There's another monster up ahead! Look! A tree monster!"

Engraved with the face of a human on its trunk, two human-faced trees are coming this way.

"Perfect! Just you wait, stumpies!"

Unsheathing his sword, Mash runs as fast as he can, but he's no match for the speed of the phoenix in the sky. It quickly swoops down and crashes into the trees, setting them ablaze before Mash can even get close. He stops, then simply stares in astonishment. However, I scream to Elulu:

"Look! There are more behind you!"

Charging toward us is a swarm of killer ants the size of human children.

"Elulu! You should be able to use Fire Arrow and hit them from here! The phoenix just exploded, too, so now's your chance!"

"O-okay!"

Elulu immediately uses Fire Arrow.

"Take thiiis!"

Moments before the arrow hits the ants, another phoenix suddenly descends in front of the spell and easily knocks it away with one of its wings before ramming into the ants, resulting in a huge blaze.

Elulu is stunned. Seiya stands by her side with his arms crossed, a look of satisfaction on his face.

"You're wasting your time. Automatic Phoenix will instantly kill all monsters under level thirty, and there are always three of them on standby in the sky. So neither of you needs to do anything."

"B-but then I'll never get to fight any monsters."

Seiya glares at Mash's sour face.

"What's wrong, Mash? I told you before. There is no greater option than winning without fighting."

"O-oh yeah! I forgot!"

"Worry less about fighting and more about keeping those items safe. Got it?"

"Y-yes, master!"

Seiya swiftly takes the lead once again.

I stare at his large back in disgust.

…No wonder we haven't been running into any monsters. Those phoenixes have been killing all of them for us. But at the very least, I really wish he would let Mash and Elulu fight just a little… A-anyway, I wonder how high Seiya's stats are right now? I mean, I had no idea he could use such a high-level long-range magic spell like that. But it's not like he'd tell me if I asked, so…

All right, it's been a while! Let's have a little peek!
I decide to use Scan on Seiya.

SEIYA RYUUGUUIN

LV: 1

HP: 111   **MP: 111**

ATK: 1   **DEF: 1**   **SPD: 1**   **MAG: 1**   **GRW: 1**

Resistance: Fire, Ice, Wind, Water, Lightning, Earth

Special Abilities: Fire Magic (LV: 1), Magic Sword (LV: 1)

Personality: Overly Cautious

E-everything's 1! This is clearly Fake Out at work! Hmph! It puts a lot of strain on my eyes, but it seems I'm just going to have to use my Goddess Power and look right through your tricks! Ready or not, here I come!

Goddess Power!

…Wh-what the…?

Before I know it, the 1s on Seiya's status screen are forming a single line. The finger-width 1s are wiggling their bodies as if they are alive while giving adorable cries.

Wh-what's going on? They…*pfft*… Th-they are kind of cute, tho—

All of a sudden, a few handfuls of 1s lunge toward my eyes! And they repeatedly poke me with their pointy tips!

"Gyaaaaah! My eyes! My eeeeeeyes!"

The pain is so unbearable that I scream, causing Mash, who's walking by my side, to jump.

"R-Rista?! What the hell! You startled me!"

"Th-the ones…! I thought they were so cute, but then they started stabbing me in the eyesss!"

"…?! Is that some kind of fairy tale or something?! Rista, you didn't smoke any strange leaves, right?!"

"I'm not having a 'bad trip' if that's what you're asking!"

Hearing the commotion, Seiya looks back and gives me a cold stare.

"…You just love peeping, huh?"

"Can you not make me sound like a criminal?!"

"Looking at someone's personal information without their consent is a crime. If there were police in this world, I'd have reported you immediately."

"I-if you don't want me looking, then just tell me what your stats are!"

"No. There's no reason for you to know. And just so you know, that trap was a warning. The next time you try that, you can say good-bye to your eyes *and* your head."

Not only my eyes but my head, too?! *Gulp…!* I sh-should probably refrain from looking for a while!

Shuddering, I give up on using Scan on Seiya.

Down the path, I begin to see a rural area up ahead with wooden huts scattered around the fields. It looks like we've arrived at a small village.

"Perfect. Let's stock up on items here. It doesn't look like they'll have much, though."

Within seconds, a middle-aged man with a beaming smile and a hoe in hand walks over to Seiya.

"Howdy, travelers. Welcome to Izale village."

Seiya drips holy water from his pocket on the man's face.

"Pff! What do you think yer doin', boy?!"

"He's human."

"Seiya?! Isn't it about time to retire the holy water?! Deathmagla's gone, so I really doubt there will be any more undead!"

"Or maybe that's what they want us to think. Never let your guard down."

Seiya then looks back at Mash.

"Mash, I'm only going to say it once, so listen carefully. There's an old saying that goes like this: 'Undead strike when you least expect it.'"

"'Undead strike when you least expect it'… Man! That's so cool!"

Wh-what's so cool about that? Is that even an old saying?

The middle-aged man looks as annoyed as I do as he stares at his holy water–drenched clothes.

"I'm soaking wet… The boy's lost his damn mind."

"Hey, you. Where's this town's item shop? Spit it out."

"Did yer mother not teach ya any manners? *Sigh*. Go straight down that path, then take a right."

We go straight down the path just like the sulking man told us. It isn't long before we find the sign to the item shop.

Elulu curiously tilts her head.

"Hmm? We're at the item shop already? But weren't we supposed to take a right?"

"I dunno. The sign says the item shop's right here."

"I bet he lied to us because he was pissed off at Seiya for pouring holy water on him."

We walk into the store. However, something immediately feels off to me the moment I set foot inside. Seiya places a finger on the sheath at his waist, apparently noticing as well.

"Welcome," calls a man with a hoarse voice, presumably the owner, from the other side of the stocked display shelf. He is extremely short with buck teeth, but there's a faint aura I can sense coming from him…

I stop Seiya, who's getting ready to draw his sword.

"S-Seiya, wait! He's a dwarf! While he might be classified as a monster, most of them don't attack humans and live peaceful lives!"

Hearing my voice echo throughout the shop, an old woman of the same short stature comes rushing over with a little boy. Their eyes open wide the moment they see Seiya with his sword unsheathed.

"P-please don't! What did my husband do to you?!"

"Stop!! Leave Papa alone!"

A young dwarf, so short that he comes up only to my knees, pleads with Seiya. He sheathes his sword, perhaps sensing no malice in them. Then he asks the frightened dwarf, "Hey. Do you have any torches here?"

"Y-yes, we do. But…are you by any chance planning on going to that cave?"

"You know it?"

"Yes, there is a cave in the rocky area to the east. However, it's a dead end the moment you walk inside."

Mash slaps his knee.

"That's it! If Elulu and I break the seal, we'll probably be able to go through the so-called dead end!"

"I see. Anyway, I'll take some torches."

"H-hey, Seiya? I was thinking. Wouldn't you just be able to use your fire magic and skip the whole torch thing?"

"No. I don't want to waste any MP."

Thereupon, Elulu energetically raises her hand.

"Th-then, Seiya, how about we use my fire magic? It doesn't matter if we waste my MP, right?"

Seiya immediately shuts her down.

"No thanks. I trust the torches to do a better job than you will."

"Seiya! I—I can't believe you!"

When I yell at him, Elulu awkwardly smiles.

"I-it's fine, Ristie. He's right. My fire is unpredictable."

"Elulu…"

I feel so bad for her. She's just trying to be helpful.

Ugh! That Seiya…! What's wrong with Elulu helping out a little?!

But Seiya is already ready to purchase the torches. He takes a few gold coins out of his pouch while turning his gaze to Mash.

"Mash, this is our first time going to a cave. Now, here's my question: How many torches do we need?"

"Fifty!"

"Mash?!"

I shout his name, taken aback by the excessive number he immediately blurted out.

Th-this kid has been poisoned by Seiya! He has no normal concept of items anymore! But even then, Seiya shakes his head.

"You were close, but no. The cave could be built like a maze, so it is safe to say that once we're inside, it could be a few weeks before we get out. Plus, we can assume there will be monsters that spit water at us and ruin the torches we're holding. In addition, we have to have enough torches to get us out of the cave after getting the ultimate weapon as well. Therefore, at the very least, we'll need around five hundred—"

"We'll take five!"

I talk over Seiya and place an order.

*   *   *

Clearly unhappy, Seiya practically has to be shoved out of the store. Full of smiles, the owner, his wife, and child see us off after we're outside.

"Thank you for your business! Travelers, may the grace of Krosde Thanatus be with you."

Krosde...? I've never heard of him before. Is that some kind of spirit worshipped around here or something?

Without putting much thought into it, we head to the next shop to pick up nonperishables and water, and soon, we're finally prepared to go to the Dragons' Den.

CHAPTER 24
Dragons' Den

We head east after leaving the village. Just like the shop owner mentioned, the terrain gradually becomes rocky until we find ourselves no longer walking on a grass field but a rocky expanse with stones of all sizes littering the ground.

More importantly, this rocky area is massive... I should have asked that shopkeeper for more details on the location of the cave.

Elulu suddenly shows me her hand.

"Ristie, look."

A crest shaped like a dragon illuminates the back of her hand. The same crest is shining on the back of Mash's hand as well.

"Heh. I've never been here, but I can feel it. The cave is that way."

Seiya and I advance with Mash and Elulu leading the way. They soon stop before a gigantic stone wall as high as the eye can see. A gaping hole slowly begins to open at the bottom.

"Looks like we're here."

Seiya takes out a torch and lights it. From here on, he takes the lead as we walk into the cave. Seiya slowly treks through the cave ever so cautiously until we reach a dead end a mere fifty or so steps in.

"Ah! See?! We're at the end already! I knew we weren't going to need those torches," I say with a smug look on my face.

However...

"Who cares? Look at this."

Seiya points at the stone wall right before us.

O-oh, so it's not important when you *make a mistake, huh?!*

I'm beyond annoyed to the point that I actually wish I could have a personality like his!

Anyway, a large mural of the dragonkin crest is painted on the wall. Underneath the painting are two handprints, making it obvious what Mash and Elulu need to do to break the seal.

"You ready, Elulu? Let's do this!"

"Ready when you are!"

As they're about to place their hands over the prints, I suddenly hear something like cracking bones coming from Seiya's direction. Everyone turns to him only to see that he has his platinum sword unsheathed before the enormous stone wall.

"S-Seiya?!"

He begins slashing relentlessly at the sturdy wall so quickly that each strike leaves a blur like Phoenix Drive. The screeching echo is so unbearable that I want to cover my ears.

"Seiya! What are you…?"

I try to stop Seiya, but…I soon find myself captivated by him. He viciously pounds at the bare rock as if he was swinging a whip, making perfect crescent motions. I've never seen such graceful and gorgeous yet fierce swordsmanship. Seiya isn't even getting winded.

"…By intensely limbering my arm and wrist joints, I am able to strike horizontally, vertically, diagonally, and straight all in one attack. Then I repeat as necessary. The name of this skill is…"

Out of nowhere, a fissure appears in the solid rock! And in the blink of an eye, the wall in front of us comes crumbling down with a heavy crash.

"…Eternal Sword."

However, Mash and Elulu are even more amazed than I am after seeing Adenela's special move.

"The hell?! He broke the seal with brute force!"

"H-he didn't even need us!"

Seiya walks ahead, ignoring the heartbroken dragonkin children.

*   *   *

After I cheer up Mash and Elulu, we follow Seiya through the hole…and are greeted by a rather disappointing sight. I was expecting there to be a big treasure chest or something, but it's just some narrow room.

"Wh-what the…? I thought the ultimate weapon was supposed to be here."

I look around but find nothing. The only noteworthy aspect of the chamber is a magic circle etched into the ground. Just as I'm about to curse our rotten luck, the magic circle begins emitting a radiant light, which is then followed by a dignified greeting.

"How far you've come, brethren. Truly, the blood of dragons is strong within you."

"Wh-what the…?!"

The male voice seems to be coming from the magic circle.

"Young Hero…come forth. Please stand atop the magic circle. In so doing, the door to Dragon Village shall open. There, you shall receive the ultimate weapon: Igzasion."

Igzasion…! So this is the ultimate weapon that can defeat the Demon Lord!

"Guys, this is probably just like the gates I create. The magic circle will teleport us to their village!"

"Dragon Village…! That must be where we're originally from, Elulu."

"Y-yeah! I'm so excited!"

"Then there's no time to waste!"

Moments before we step on the magic circle, Seiya extends his arm and stops us.

"Wait. It's too dangerous. It's probably a trap."

"Huh…? A trap…? Seiya?"

Seiya catches a lizard crawling on the wall, then places it on the magic circle.

"All right, we're on the magic circle."

Then he blatantly lies while facing the magic circle.

What?! But we're not! That's a lizard!

"Very well. Then I shall warp you to Dragon Village."

The lizard is immediately showered in light before disappearing as if it were absorbed by the magic circle. Before long, a dignified yet somewhat confused voice echoes from the magic circle.

"Um... There appears to be a lizard here, but..."

"Good. Now send that lizard back here."

"B-but why would you...?"

"Just do it. Don't tell me you can't."

"V-very well..."

A few moments go by before the lizard is sent back, which Seiya watches with interest.

"Hmm… There doesn't seem to be anything wrong with it. It appears this isn't a trap to teleport us to another dimension to dispose of us."

"...I–I wouldn't...d-do something like that..."

The once-dignified voice of the magic circle now sounds flustered.

…Eventually Seiya deems the magic circle safe enough for us to use, and we get teleported.

"Welcome to Dragon Village."

I turn in the direction of the voice—the same one emanating from the circle…

"Eek!"

…and scream.

He's standing on two legs like a human and wearing hemp clothes, but…he's a giant lizard. Small fangs grow from his protruding mouth, which produces human speech.

"I don't blame you for being surprised. We dragonewts look quite different from humans, after all."

The dragonewt narrows his reptilian eyes while skewing his lips. I'm guessing he's trying to smile.

"However, you aren't the only ones surprised. I wasn't expecting to welcome a tiny lizard to the village."

"Y-yeah, we're really sorry about that."

The dragonewt giggles.

"Well, I feel a lot safer knowing that we're leaving the fate of the world in the hands of someone so cautious… Oh, I forgot to introduce myself. I am Lagos, protector of the Dragons' Den."

Lagos walks ahead and reaches for the door to the room.

"Now come, the Great Mother of Dragons awaits you in the sanctuary. Allow me to guide you."

Once outside, we find ourselves in the middle of a city, but it's different from any village or town we've ever seen in Gaeabrande. It's called Dragon Village, so I was expecting someplace more pastoral. Instead, it's closer to the unified spirit world. If I was to compare it to Seiya's world, I'd say it's very baroque with elaborate and artistic architecture.

Lagos leads the way while we try to take in all the unique sights.

"Our village is on the continent of Yulea to the far west across the ocean from where you were. Yulea is a phantasmal continent unreachable by humans. The only way they can access these lands is through that magic circle."

…Interesting. Dragons are close to deities in all worlds, it seems. As long as there isn't any trouble in the human world, they live in secrecy and keep to themselves.

As Lagos leads us to the sanctuary, some dragonewts we pass speak up when they see Mash and Elulu.

"Is that Lord Mash and Lady Elulu?!"

"Lord Mash! Look how strong he's become!"

"Yes, and Lady Elulu grew up to be such a beautiful woman as well!"

Fully aware of the dragonewts' envious gazes, Mash strikes up a conversation with Lagos to hide his embarrassment.

"H-hey, so…why do Elulu and I look so different from everyone here?"

"We dragonewts descended from both humans and dragons. However, for most of us, our dragon side is more dominant due to having more dragon blood than human."

Then Seiya chimes in.

"So these two are failures without much dragon blood?"

"We are?!"

"We…are…?!"

Mash and Elulu fall into depression, but before I can chew Seiya out, Lagos gives a hearty laugh.

"No, no, no! Quite the opposite, actually! Lord Mash and Lady Elulu are the chosen ones! They are destined to perform great acts that normal dragonewts are incapable of!"

"Like what?"

But Lagos shakes his head in response to Mash's question.

"You should hear that directly from the Great Mother of Dragons herself."

After Lagos falls silent, Elulu suddenly asks:

"Hey, Lagos, do we have any family around here? L-like a mom or dad…?"

Seconds of silence go by until…

"It truly pains me to tell you this, but…both of your parents passed away over a decade ago due to an epidemic in our village. From what I've heard, this epidemic tragically claimed the rest of your family as well…"

"O-oh…"

"Elulu… Are you okay?"

"I-I'm fine! I figured as much! Besides, I have Mash!"

Lagos smiles at Elulu as she does her best to act cheerful.

"Please think of everyone here as your family. In fact, the Great Mother is everyone's mother, in a way. She is really looking forward to seeing you two."

"Really? I can't wait to meet her!"

Elulu's smile returns.

The Great Mother of Dragons… I wonder if she's noble and kind to every-one like Ishtar is to us goddesses?

Lagos ends up bringing us to a luxuriously built sanctuary that rivals that of the spirit world. At the end of an excessively long red carpet sits the Great Mother, the queen of dragons, surrounded by her dragonewt atten-dants. Perhaps noticing our arrival, she slowly stands from her seat.

"You've come a long way. I am the ruler of Dragon Village, the Great Mother of Dragons."

Her voice alone reveals her nobility. She wears an expensive-looking necklace and an olive-green dress that trails on the ground. However, from what little I can see, her skin is ocher and reptilian. She has a cold gaze that is impossible to read and a protruding nose and mouth.

The Great Mother, standing upright, looks no different from any of the other giant lizard-like dragonewts.

Er… She's nothing like Ishtar. And calling her beautiful…would be a crime.

Her reptilian eyes open wide while she speaks with a note of seriousness.

"Now then, the situation is urgent. Precisely as the late Yellow Dragon Emperor foretold one hundred years ago, evil is starting to swallow this world. The Demon Lord has established his domain in the frozen northern continent of Alphoreiz, and he is steadily expanding his territory even as we speak."

The moment I hear that, I raise my voice.

"The continent of Alphoreiz…! So that's where the Demon Lord is!"

I put my long-held idea into words.

"Now that we know where the Demon Lord's castle is, we could just use Seiya's Meteor Strike to take him out!"

But the Great Mother shakes her head.

"That won't work. The outside of the enormous castle is protected by Reflect, so if you try to hit it with a meteor, it will bounce back and hit the caster."

O-oh… I guess it's not going to be that easy…

"But do not fear. That is why we have Mash and Elulu, after all."

She squints while looking at them, then motions Mash to approach.

"Mash, come here."

"Huh?! M-me?"

After he timidly makes his way to the Great Mother, she places a hand on his head.

"I shall teach you how to transform."

In a flash, her hand begins to glow. And then, right before our eyes…

"M-Mash?!"

The skin on his face, arms, and legs begins to turn ocher! His body and face change as well…

"Wh-wh-what the…?! What's happening to me?!"

By the time Mash cries out, he's already a full-fledged lizardman—er…I mean…a dragonewt!

"Someone bring us a mirror."

As Mash gazes into the hand mirror one of the attendants gave him…

"Wha—?"

He bemoans the man he has become. The Great Mother follows with a laugh.

"Hoh-hoh… I know it must be a surprise to see yourself like that all of a sudden. However, Mash, you are far stronger now than you once were."

"R-really? …Rista! Can you check for me?"

"O-okay!"

I use Scan and immediately swallow my breath.

MASH

LV: 16

HP: 1,381   **MP: 0**

ATK: 9,210   **DEF: 8,770**   **SPD: 7,900**   **MAG: 0**   **GRW: 57**

Resistance: Fire, Ice, Poison

Special Abilities: ATK Boost (LV: 5), Dragonewt Metamorphosis (LV: 3)

Skills: Dragon Thrust, Dragon Slash

Personality: Brave

…His level hasn't changed, but…

"M-Mash! Your attributes are ten times better now!"

"B-but now that you mention it…I feel like I can do anything!"

While originally upset about the change in appearance, the current Mash swells with pride.

"Master, look how strong I've become!"

"Indeed. Don't get too close, though. I might mistake you for a monster and kill you."

"…?! Hey! Who are you calling a monster?!"

"Still, this is a surprise. Good job, Mash."

Mash seems really happy to be complimented by Seiya for a change, but…

"Now your attributes are about one-thirtieth of mine."

The casual statement is a gut punch to Mash's self-esteem.

"What…? They're only one-thirtieth of yours…? Even after transforming into a dragonewt? Y-you've gotta be kidding me…"

And just like that, Mash returns to his human form in low spirits. Seiya pats him on the shoulder, oblivious to his feelings.

"Congratulations, Mash. Now you can carry even more stuff."

"Th-thanks…"

H-he was so happy to be ten times stronger…only for this to happen. I feel so sorry for him…

Wait a second. Seiya is thirty times stronger than that? Just how strong is this Hero?!

The Great Mother cheerfully smiles at Mash, as down as he is.

"Mash, continue training, and when the time comes, you will be able to transform from a dragonewt into a dragon god, becoming exponentially stronger than before."

"R-really?!"

"Of course. You are the chosen one of the dragonkin. A great power sleeps within you."

"Yes!! I'm gonna train so hard!"

As Mash's heart fills with hope and dreams, Elulu cries out, unable to endure the feeling of getting left behind any longer.

"G-Great Mother…! C-can you do that to me, too?!"

"That will not be necessary for you, Elulu."

"What…?! B-but…"

Elulu is on the verge of tears, having been pushed away by not only Seiya but the Great Mother of Dragons as well. However, the queen affectionately reassures her:

"Do not worry. You have an important mission that awaits you—one even greater than Mash's."

"R-really?! What kind of mission?!"

As Elulu's eyes sparkle in wonder, the queen sticks out her long, forked red tongue.

"Elulu, you shall give your life for the holy sword—Igzasion."

CHAPTER 25
Ritual of the Holy Sword

"…!"

Elulu freezes. Even Mash is at a loss for words.

I look to the Great Mother of Dragons, doubting my ears.

"Um… Wh-what was that?"

"Hmm? This girl, Elulu, is destined to become Igzasion."

"Wh-what the hell does that even mean?! I-isn't Igzasion supposed to be a weapon?!"

"It is. Igzasion is a holy sword with unparalleled powers to defeat the Demon Lord. It is born in the form of a human and will only truly manifest in this world through the sacrifice of a dragonkin girl."

The queen's voice is bereft of concern as she relays this horrifying fact as if talking about the weather.

"By spending over a decade in the human world, Elulu has bathed in vital energies, becoming a perfect vessel for Igzasion. I truly envy you, Elulu. You shall become the key to saving this world. You shall live on forever as the holy sword Igzasion. You are the pride of our people."

The queen and all the attendants behind her smile, showing their small fangs.

"Now, I shall start preparing for the ritual of the holy sword. The ritual shall take place tonight after the last supper. Elulu, spend as much time as you can with your friends until then."

*   *   *

After that, we leave the sanctuary as if our souls have been stolen. Nobody says a word. We just wander around Dragon Village in a daze. After some time goes by, Mash finally speaks as if having made up his mind.

"Elulu… What are we going to do?"

"Wh-what do you mean?"

"What do you think I mean?! I'm talking about you dying and becoming Igzasion! Are you seriously okay with that?!"

Elulu looks slightly troubled, then says:

"…If that's my destiny, then that's my destiny."

"You can't be serious!"

Elulu giggles.

"But you know what? I've always wanted to do something for you all! I want to be useful! That's why I'm actually kind of happy my wish is coming true! Plus, I get to live forever as a sword, and I can even save the world!"

"Elulu…"

As Mash lowers his gaze, Elulu looks at me.

"This is right, isn't it?! I'm doing the right thing, right, Ristie?!"

"Y-yeah…"

I offer reluctant reassurance.

…I came to Gaeabrande as a goddess to save it. So if one of our party members needs to give their life for the cause, shouldn't I willingly accept? Elulu herself says she's prepared to die. But…

…Is this… Is this really okay?

No matter how much I think about it, I can't find any answers—only frustration.

Despite being a goddess, I turn to Seiya—a human—for advice.

"H-hey, Seiya… How about saying som—? Huh…?"

When I look in Seiya's direction, I find myself at a loss for words. He's chatting with a dragonewt selling items down the street.

"Sir, feast your eyes on this! It's called a speed seed! You eat it, and it'll increase your speed for ten minutes! You won't find these in any human town!"

"Can you really eat these?"

"You can eat as many as you want!"

"You better not be lying to me. I'll sue you."

"Well, aren't you a skeptic! But I swear to the god of my village, you'll be fine!"

"I guess I'll take some, then."

"S-Seiya! What do you think you're doing, shopping at a time like this?!"

I start chewing him out, but he isn't listening. He takes a few gold coins out of his pouch, then pays for the items before finally turning around and acknowledging my existence.

"What?"

"Don't give me that! Don't you have something to say to Elulu?"

Thereupon, Seiya turns his sharp, piercing gaze on Elulu.

"She already knows what she needs to do. She doesn't need me telling her."

Mm…

It's as if he has no qualms about the situation at all, just like the Great Mother, but even then, I can't believe how easily he comes to a decision.

There's a hint of sorrow in Elulu's smile.

"Y-yeah, he's right. It goes without saying, doesn't it?! Ha-ha! Yeah, Seiya's right!"

…I get it. It must be done to save the world. And most of all, if Elulu herself is prepared to do it…

Before I even realize, it starts getting dark, and a group of armored dragonewts drop to one knee in front of us.

"The last supper has been prepared. Allow us to guide you to the Dragon Gorge. This way, please."

As the sun disappears over the horizon, we traverse the steep mountain slope until we reach an area near the valley illuminated by torches. There are numerous wooden tables and chairs lined up. On the tables are plates of steaming hot food and expensive-looking grape wine. A few dozen dragonewts are pleasantly chatting at the tables. The queen is sitting at an even more luxurious table and enjoying her own glass of wine. Noticing our arrival, she motions us over.

"Come, come, have a seat. Goddess, Hero, Mash—this way."

When Elulu tries to join us, an armored dragonewt blocks her path.

"Lady Elulu, we've prepared a change of clothes for you over here. This way, please."

"E-Elulu…!"

Mash extends an arm but can't reach her. She worriedly glances back at Mash while the dragonewt takes her away. Then, all of a sudden, the Great Mother powerfully claps her hands together with a *bang*.

"Now let us feast until Elulu has finished changing."

The dragonewt guards push Mash and me by the shoulders, forcing us into our seats.

"Our villagers put their hearts and souls into the preparation of this food. I hope you enjoy it."

"Th-thanks…"

I'm not the least bit hungry, so I reach out for light foods such as soup and salad. From the look on his face, Mash begins sipping his soup out of politeness. However, Seiya doesn't touch his food, drinking only the water he brought himself. Young dragonewts swarm him with plates of food.

"Hey, we made cookies! Try one!"

The three children are much more adorable than their adult counterparts, and seeing them makes me feel slightly at ease. I smile as I take a cookie.

"Mister, you too! Try one! We worked really hard to bake them!"

Seiya reluctantly picks up a cookie. Then, as if he noticed I was glaring at him to make sure he wouldn't say anything awful to these innocent children, he munches on it in silence.

While eating the cookie, I timidly try talking to the queen as she drinks her wine.

"H-hey, uh… Does Elulu *have* to become the sword?"

"Of course. There is no other way to save the world. If she doesn't, then the Demon Lord will destroy everything."

"O-oh… Yeah… Of course…"

"Now, you need to focus on enjoying this banquet. This is for Elulu's sake, after all."

"O-okay…"

Dragonewts dance around the tables to the beat of the drums and flute. When the dance ends, the torches that lit up the area all go out at once, and complete darkness takes over. However, within seconds, torches reignite to demarcate a single path to the valley. Escorted by a dragonewt and dressed in a gorgeous light-crimson dress, Elulu slowly walks between the torches. Her red hair is neatly worn up, accenting her makeup. Around her neck hangs a lavish pendant given to her by the Great Mother of Dragons. Elulu has a dignified beauty to her, akin to that of a noblewoman.

The queen rises from her seat.

"Now, let the holy sword ritual begin."

She points to the valley, the end of Elulu's path.

"At the bottom of the valley, in the Abyss, lies a magic circle created by the Yellow Dragon Emperor long ago. Once the destined child, Elulu, leaps into it, her flesh and blood will be absorbed, and she will transform into the radiant holy sword Igzasion."

Every dragonewt in attendance gives a round of applause and cheers. Bathing in their thunderous applause, Elulu walks to the Abyss. When she is finally only steps from the valley, Mash and I are unable to stay quiet any longer.

"Elulu!"

"E-Elulu! Wait!!"

Elulu looks back and smiles with tears in her eyes.

"G-good-bye, Mash. Good-bye, Ristie! Bye, Seiya! M-make sure you treat me well after I become a sword! Ha-ha… M-make sure you polish me sometimes so I don't get rusty!"

The Great Mother yells out.

"The time has come, Elulu! Throw yourself into the Abyss!"

The cheers get even louder. Mash trembles by my side.

"Th-this isn't right…! This isn't right!"

"M-Mash?"

"This isn't how it's supposed to be!"

Mash makes a dash for Elulu, but the armored guards grab him as if they were expecting this to happen.

"Lord Mash, control yourself!"

"You mustn't interrupt the ritual!"

He curses while being held down by the armored guards...

"D-dammit!"

Then Mash screams to me.

"Rista! Don't tell me you're okay with this! Do you really think this is right...?!"

"...!"

I'm at a loss for words.

O-of course I don't want to see Elulu die! But this world will perish without Igzasion! Wh-what should I do?!

At a complete loss, I look over at Elulu...

"M-Mash...! Rista...! I—I...! I...!"

She's scared. Tears are welling up in her eyes. Her resolution is wavering. The queen looks at Elulu with a dubious glare.

"Oh dear. It appears that their cries weakened your resolve. This isn't good. This isn't good at all. Could somebody give Elulu some help?"

A dragonewt a great deal larger than all the rest approaches Elulu.

The Great Mother of Dragons turns her cold reptilian eyes toward her.

"Now throw her into the Abyss."

"Wh-what?! Wait! This is no different from murder now!"

But my words are drowned out by the dragonewts' feverish excitement.

"Oh, what a wonderful day!"

"Fall into the Abyss!"

"Die and become Igzasion!"

"This is your destiny, Lady Elulu!"

"This is for the sake of the world!"

Their madness and excitement fill the air. In the midst of the insanity is when I realize—it's too late to save Elulu. Blocked by dragonewts, I helplessly watch Elulu trembling in fright. A brawny hand reaches out to push her into the Abyss from behind.

However...

"Gwaaah?!"

Before the dragonewt's hand can even touch Elulu, he is knocked back a few dozen meters and comes crashing through the queen's table.

"Wh-what's going on?!"

The Great Mother shrieks in surprise. Absolute silence reigns over the banquet. Everyone's eyes are on the Hero, slowly lowering his extended leg from the air.

Mash, Elulu, and I stare at him in blank amazement. Then Elulu opens her quivering mouth and asks:

"S-Seiya? Why...?"

"Do I have to repeat myself? You don't need me to tell you... Tsk. Are you really that dense?"

After uttering a sigh, Seiya casually says, "Your job is to carry my stuff. How are you supposed to do that if you're a sword?"

CHAPTER 26
Death Sentence

The dragonewt spectators are at a loss for words, as are the queen, Mash, and even Elulu, who stands stock-still.

I've grown somewhat used to Seiya's behavior through personal experience, but I can't help but ask:

"S-Seiya… That's what you meant when you said she doesn't need you telling her what to do…?"

"Of course. I said before that these two will be carrying my stuff from now on, didn't I? Nothing has changed."

"B-but…like…we're not going to be able to save the world if Elulu doesn't become Igzasion, you know?"

Seiya snorts with a "humph."

"Even with that Igzasion or whatever, there's no guarantee it'd really be able to kill the Demon Lord."

As expected, the Great Mother of Dragons cannot contain herself any longer.

"Blasphemy! The holy sword Igzasion shall become a weapon of unrivaled might, surpassing even the Demon Lord's, once it absorbs her life, flesh, and blood!"

"How can you be so sure?"

"Because the Yellow Dragon Emperor's divine messages from one hundred years ago are absolute!"

"That's not the least bit logical."

After deeply sighing, Seiya regards the queen as one might garbage.

"…In the end, they're nothing more than the nonsensical words of some dumb lizard."

"What?! Wh-who do you think you're talking to?! Hold your tongue, Hero!"

Th-the nonsensical words of some dumb lizard…? I—I worried so much over those words, Elulu fell into despair, and Mash became furious…but that's all they were to Seiya?

Slightly fed up, I stare at his profile.

Seriously… This Hero never changes…

All of a sudden, I feel something welling from the depths of my stomach, and I open my mouth.

"Ha-ha… Ha-ha-ha!"

A fit of laughter.

"What?! What's so funny?!"

The queen turns her gaze to me, scowling fiercely.

"O-oh! My apologies!"

"I am afraid to ask, but do you share the Hero's sentiment? You are not telling me that you do not wish to defeat the Demon Lord and save the world, correct?"

In the face of her threatening attitude…

"We want nothing more than to defeat the Demon Lord and save this world. However…"

I strain my voice so as to not fall victim to the Great Mother's intimidation, then declare:

"However, we will not sacrifice our friend to do so! We will find another way to defeat the Demon Lord without Igzasion!"

The area falls silent. A few moments pass until the Great Mother glares at me disdainfully.

"…So you've made up your mind. A foolish goddess for a foolish Hero."

She raises her gooseneck and points at Elulu with the tip of her nose.

"You are no different from this girl's family. 'Please, she's our daughter,' 'Please, she's our friend…' You cannot think outside of your small, insignificant world. They would still be alive today were it not for their selfish views."

That inexcusable remark elicits a reaction from Mash even before Elulu.

"The hell are you talkin' about?! I thought our families died during the epidemic?!"

"A little over ten years ago after Elulu's birth, we decided to send her to the human world to make her a vessel for Igzasion. However, her parents rebelled, as did your family with whom they were close. That is why…"

She sticks out her long tongue, licking her lips.

"…I had them killed."

Elulu covers her mouth when she hears the startling revelation.

"H-how could you?! Why…?!"

"How awful…"

I glare in disgust, but the Great Mother of Dragons is unapologetic.

"It had to be done for the good of the world."

"UUURRAAAAAGGH!"

With a furious roar, Mash transforms into a dragonewt while still pinned down. After the awesome power knocks away the two dragonewts, he immediately lunges toward the queen with a growl.

"And they call you the Mother of Dragons?! What bullshit! You're nothing more than a murderer!"

He raises his fist into the air while rushing toward the queen, but his legs suddenly begin to falter, as if he was intoxicated, before ultimately collapsing beneath him.

"Wha—?!"

"Mash?!"

I try running over to him, but my legs also give out, causing me to flop to the ground on my stomach.

"Wh-what's…going…on?"

With venom in her eyes, the Great Mother looks down at us crawling on the ground, then laughs.

"Hmm-hmm-hmm… I've grown cautious in my old age. When I told you that Elulu would become Igzasion, I saw your reactions and had a feeling it would come to this. Therefore, I had some paralyzing potions mixed into your food. They will not kill you, but they're powerful mixtures that cannot be cured with spells or items. Even a goddess will be immobilized for some time."

Tsk! Paralyzing potions…! That rotten lizard…! She's just as bad as the monsters in this world! B-but we have Seiya on our side! He'll save us!

But the dragonewt children standing before Mash and me snicker.

"Ha-ha-ha! We poured some paralyzing potion into our cookies as well!"

Wh-what?! Seiya ate one of those cookies, too! Wh-which means…none of us can move right now!

"…Now that that has been taken care of, let us continue the ritual. Someone come throw Elulu down into the Abyss."

Three dragonewts begin closing in on Elulu. She's terrified. However, there is nothing that Mash, Seiya, or I can do but clench our teeth and watch her get pushed into the Abyss…

Or so I thought… Mouth agape, I gawk at the scene unfolding before me. Wearing a composed expression, Seiya casually tosses the dragonewts pursuing Elulu aside with one hand!

The queen's face turns red as she raises her voice.

"Wh-why?! Why isn't the potion working on you?!"

"Why would it? I never ate anything in the first place."

The Hero's composed explanation sends the kids into a rage.

"L-liar! You ate one of the cookies we made!"

"While you may be kids, do you really think I'd eat anything made by a lizard? Disgusting. I secretly spit it out when you weren't looking."

"…?! Y-you jerk!"

"I'm the jerk? You little shits, I knew they were poisoned. Besides…"

Seiya suddenly points at me.

"…for the most part, I only eat what she makes me."

…I know now is the absolute worst time, but my heart just skipped a beat.

S-Seiya?! Do you know how happy it makes me to hear you say that?! Ahhh… I feel like the luckiest wife in the world! I mean, I'm not a wife, but still…! Seiya, you're so dreeeamy!

Anyway, the Great Mother's initial surprise slowly fades. She snorts aggressively from the small nostrils on her snout.

"Well, you've left me with no choice. You will be the wielder of the holy sword, so I cannot be too rough, but this is for the holy ritual. I will have to silence you for a bit."

"Oh? Go ahead and try."

"I admire your confidence. However, you would be a fool to underestimate me."

The queen's dress suddenly splits open, tearing to shreds as she grows!

"Allow me to show you an ability only the chosen dragonkin can perform—Dragon God Metamorphosis!"

"Wh-wh-what the…?!"

Fearful of being squished, I struggle to move my paralyzed body and am somehow able to back away from the Great Mother.

Her transformation isn't gradual but instantaneous. The lizard body for which she'd been ridiculed has mutated into a colossal dragon with ocher scales. I'm guessing her body spans roughly ten meters in length with her long, thick tail included. The Great Mother spreads her massive wings and lifts her head into the air, exposing her ferocious face. Then she opens her mouth, baring her knifelike fangs, and roars.

Squirming on the ground, I use Scan to check her status.

GREAT MOTHER OF DRAGONS

LV: 66

HP: 563,290   MP: 5,533

ATK: 43,898   DEF: 38,881   SPD: 5,679   MAG: 10,209   GRW: 721

Resistance: Fire, Water, Lightning, Poison, Paralysis, Sleep, Curse, Instant Death, Status Ailments

Special Abilities: Dragon God Metamorphosis (LV: MAX) *Only takes physical damage from weapons strong against dragon-type enemies

Skills: Dragon Claw, Dragon Breath, Ultimate Wall

Personality: Self-righteous

…Her HP is huge! But the rest isn't that impressive compared to Dark Firus!

"Wait… She's immune to almost all physical damage?!"

The Great Mother guffaws, apparently having heard my utterance.

"Grah-ha-ha-ha! It must have never crossed your mind that you would end up fighting a dragon while you were here. The scales of a dragon are stronger than any metal! An ordinary sword won't even leave a scratch! Hero, do you know what this means? You cannot defeat me!"

"It never crossed my mind that I would be fighting a dragon…?"

Her self-aggrandizing speech doesn't even make me flinch. In fact, I gaze at the Hero with hopeful eyes.

His eyes locked on the Great Mother, Seiya calls out to Mash.

"Mash. Can you move?"

"Y-yeah… A l-little…"

"Then take my sword with the black sheath out of your bag."

Mash uses what little strength he has to retrieve the sword, then throws it to Seiya as hard as he can. Without looking, Seiya catches it with one hand and draws it on the queen.

…However, the unsheathed blade isn't his usual platinum sword.

The weapon mysteriously glows bloodred. It whirs through the air as Seiya performs movements akin to a blade dance before settling into his battle stance. Despite being many times the size of a human, the dragon quivers.

"I-it can't be… Is that the…Dragon Killer?! Wh-why do you have that?! Did you come here expecting to fight?!"

As always, without a hint of emotion, Seiya says, "I considered it more than likely that I'd have to fight a dragon the moment it was decided we were going to a place called the Dragons' Den."

I raise my arm to the Great Mother and yell:

"Ha! Seiya is always perfectly prepared! Don't underestimate an overly cautious Hero!"

Mash's eyes glitter as he gazes at Seiya in admiration.

"That's my master for ya! But where did you even get that?!"

"From synthesizing, of course. I combined a platinum sword; one of your hairs, since you're a dragonkin; one of Elulu's hairs for the same reason; and around a hundred strands of hair from Rista to make it."

I am taken aback by the ingredients used to make the Dragon Killer.

Wh-why did he need so much of *my* hair?! The situation is dire, but even then, there's something I have to ask Seiya.

"S-Seiya! How did you get so much of my hair?! There's no way you found all of it in my room!"

"Correct. That's why I took directly from the source while you were sleeping."

"…?!"

Huh? Wait. Huh?! When I was sleeping? What? He pulled the hairs straight off my head? What?

"Seiya Ryuuguuin… We are going to have a long talk after this!"

But he isn't listening—as always. He looks ahead, keeping an eye on the Great Mother's movement.

Yeah, I know. The battle is more important right now. I get it. Sure. It's fine. Please focus on the battle right now. But… But you know what? We're going to have a hearing after this, you filthy stalker! Ahhhhhh!

…Seiya and the Great Mother of Dragons stare each other down. However, the Great Mother soon makes the first move. The instant her massive front legs twitch, she lunges toward Seiya with her black claws. While keeping his eyes fixed on her movement, Seiya simply backsteps with ease. He then immediately points the Dragon Killer at her.

"Atomic Split Slash."

He swings the Dragon Killer at her still-extended front legs, and it loudly clinks like iron hitting iron. The Great Mother roars.

"Gwah! What awesome power! Though you're equipped with the Dragon Killer, I nevertheless commend you for dealing me such damage with a single strike! However…"

She gets into a fighting stance with her two front legs.

"Dragon Claw!"

Her claws grow to sword length, and she takes massive swipes at Seiya. Each strike howls through the air, generating unbelievable wind pressure. While powerful, not one attack connects with the Hero.

Yes! We actually can judge this book by its cover! Due to her large size, she's not that fast, so Seiya should have no problem with her!

I exhale a sigh of relief, but…

"Mm…"

The moment Seiya dodges her claws, he dashes straight for Elulu, snatching her up while still running. After creating some distance between himself and the Great Mother, he comes to an abrupt stop, kicking up a cloud of dust.

"Wh-what?!"

Elulu panics, unable to process what's going on. I'm also confused, but it isn't long before I figure out why Seiya grabbed Elulu and ran. I look over to the spot where she'd been standing a moment ago and see a huge engraving of the queen's claws.

There is a glow of admiration in the Great Mother's eyes.

"Oh? I was planning to gore her with my claws while pretending to attack you…but it seems you figured it out. Very impressive."

Seiya was able to somehow sense she was going to attack Elulu! Hold up…

"'Gore her'?! You mean *kill* her?! What happened to turning her into Igzasion?!"

Without missing a beat, she replies:

"Whether she dies before or after falling into the Abyss isn't important. What is important is having the flesh and blood of the chosen one absorbed by the magic circle."

"Y-you're a monster!"

But Elulu is now tucked safely in Seiya's arms. The Great Mother won't be able to get to her that easily.

However…

"I told you. I have become very cautious in my old age."

As she utters those ominous words—

"Mn… Ahhh!"

—Elulu moans in agony while clutching her chest.

"E-Elulu?!"

A black light begins emanating from the center of the necklace Elulu wears.

"Wh-what did you do to her?!"

"Heh-heh-heh… I activated the cursed item I had placed on her—the Death Sentence Necklace. Elulu's life will come to an end once the black light completely encircles her neck. She has three minutes to live."

CHAPTER 27
What's Important

"A c-cursed item?! You'd really go that far?!"

"But of course! Elulu is destined to perish and become the sword! Her fate was sealed one hundred years ago!"

Elulu tries to tear off the necklace, but it doesn't even budge. Within seconds, she clasps her chest, falls to her knees, and her breathing becomes ragged.

"You're going to pay for this!!"

Mash struggles, forcing his numb, paralyzed body into a half-sitting position, but he can't move from there. The paralysis potion is still taking effect, and I'm no different.

The black light gradually makes its way around the necklace toward Elulu's nape.

"S-Seiya…! You have to hurry!"

Time is of the essence. While I panic…

"Great Mother, you're not part of the Demon Lord's army, so I'm going to give you a chance."

…Seiya's tone is deadpan, even at a time like this.

"Lift the curse off the shrimp. After that, let us leave this village. Consider this your last warning."

"What a humorous Hero you are. A warning, you say? When I have the upper hand?"

The queen roars with laughter.

"Ha-ha-ha-ha! I refuse! The ritual of the holy sword must continue! If you want to remove her death sentence, then you will have to kill me first!"

"Is that so? Then I'll stop holding back."

The Dragon Killer in his hands glows an even darker red than before. When I see the blade engulfed in flames, I know *exactly* which magic sword skill he's going to use. Without a doubt, it's...

"Phoenix Drive!"

This is the special move Seiya used to kill Chaos Machina in the blink of an eye. But as he's about to unleash it on the Great Mother, I yell:

"Seiya, wait! She's resistant to fire ma— Huh?"

Using Flight, the Hero is already zipping around the dragon while wildly slashing at her giant body. Even with her resistance to fire, each hit scorches her scales, creating smoke.

"H-he's tearing her apart...!"

It's obvious that his attacks are hurting her, judging from the red swelling created with each hit and the queen's roars of pain.

After the Phoenix Drive rushdown ends, I use Scan once more to check how much damage she's taken.

HP: 341,577/563,290

Yes! She's already been brought down to almost half her HP just like that! He'll be able to save Elulu in time at this rate!

My heart bubbles with excitement as I witness Seiya's devastating attack power. However, the Great Mother also shows signs of admiration.

"Wonderful! Simply wonderful, Hero! I never expected you to be this strong! Once you obtain Igzasion, you stand a good chance of defeating the Demon Lord!"

Sh-she's still rambling on about that?! Give it a rest! More importantly, how can she act so confident after having almost half her HP taken away?

"You are strong...but that is still not enough...to save her."

The Great Mother suddenly changes color. The ocher scales covering her body glow with intense energy until they are completely gold, then stick out like spikes.

"Now none of your attacks can hurt me! Ultimate Wall is an unparalleled, impenetrable defense skill that cannot be broken!"

"U-unparalleled...?! Impenetrable?!"

Even as I mutter to myself, the light continues advancing around the necklace. Elulu moans in pain.

Seiya slowly points the Dragon Killer at the queen.

"I'll tear down that wall."

Y-yeah! Impenetrable? Ha! Seiya was even able to break through the ironclad defense of Dark Firus, so I'm sure he'll figure something out again!

Awash in my admiring gaze, the almighty yet careful Hero takes a small pouch out of his pocket.

"S-Seiya...? What's that?"

"It's a speed seed I bought at the item shop earlier."

"Oh, I see! You're going to use that to raise your attack speed!"

Then Seiya lifts his head back before dumping every seed in the bag into his mouth.

"...?! All of them...?"

Filled with countless seeds, Seiya's cheeks bulge.

"Ahhh! You can't say something cool like, 'I'll tear down that wall,' then make yourself look like a hamster!"

"...What's the problem?"

But when Seiya looks back at me, his cheeks are no longer puffed out. He must have chewed and swallowed the seeds really quickly.

"Now that I'm faster..."

In the blink of an eye, Seiya vanishes. My eyes dart around until I find him at something of a distance next to Mash.

Wh-whoa! It almost looked like he teleported! So this is what happens after you stuff your cheeks with so many speed seeds that you start looking like a hamster!

Seiya takes another black-sheathed sword out of Mash's bag, then draws it to reveal another red-bladed sword just like the one in his other hand.

"Dragon Killer?! You had another one?!"

"It's a spare. I didn't want to have to worry about breaking one. But sometimes spares can be used like this."

He adopts his battle stance with a Dragon Killer in each hand. Then he turns his piercing stare on the dragon.

"Mode: Double Eternal Sword!"

Oooh! Speed seeds, dual Dragon Killers, and Adenela's special move Eternal Sword…! Th-this will surely…!

"Hmph… Feel free to attack whenever you are ready, Hero."

"I'll do just that."

Seiya leaps toward the queen's bosom and strikes multiple times with both blades. Before the blur effect from one impossibly quick slash disappears, he hits her with another! His attacks are so fast that it just sounds like a continuous clinking. After a barrage of violent cuts to the stomach, the Great Mother begins moving due to the shock.

"Wh-whoa! It's working! It's working…!"

It seems like the paralysis potion is wearing off a little. After staggering to my feet, I approach Elulu and wrap her in my arms.

"Don't worry, Elulu! Seiya's going to take care of her in no time!"

"Th-thanks…!"

But just how much damage did Seiya's special attack, unrivaled in its power, do to the Great Mother?

I use Scan to check…and my heart sinks.

HP: 340,881/563,290

"Wh-what the…?! Her HP has barely changed?! B-but…!"

If memory serves, she hasn't even lost 1,000 HP since the last time I checked!

"Hmm-hmm-hmm! I told you! Ultimate Wall is the ultimate defense skill! Not only does it have zero elemental weaknesses, it is immune to all magic and physical attacks!"

The dragon grins, revealing sharp teeth.

"By the way, each of the Hero's attacks did around one to three points of damage."

"Th-that's it?!"

"He should be proud. Normally, most attacks wouldn't do any damage to Ultimate Wall. However, the Hero was able to inflict some because of the dual Dragon Killers and his immense strength, though it wasn't much."

The black light has already circled halfway around Elulu's necklace.

The Great Mother opens her mouth and brazenly announces:

"Elulu has only one minute to live! You'll have to attack even more quickly if you ever wish to defeat me! Hmm… Around two thousand hits a second would do it! Mwa-ha-ha-ha! Hero, let us put an end to this meaningless fight! There is no saving her!"

But even then, Seiya doesn't listen. He continues concentrating singlemindedly on his dual wielding strikes. Even I could tell that the attacks weren't meaningless. "A vain attempt" is the only way I could describe it.

"Seiya… I-it's okay… That's e-enough…"

"Elulu?!"

Fighting through the curse with what little strength she has left, Elulu calls out from behind Seiya.

"Thank you…for trying to save me… I'm so happy…but…you've done enough… It's okay…"

After seeing Elulu's courageous smile, the Great Mother smirks contentedly.

"It appears Elulu has given up and accepted her fate."

When I look at her necklace, the black light is only moments away from her nape. I lose my composure and tighten my arms around her.

Is this it? Not even Seiya can save her? Is becoming Igzasion really her destiny? Will we really not be able to save the S-ranked world Gaeabrande without it?

"Go, Elulu! Die and become Igzasion!"

Her voice resounds victoriously…

"…?!"

But then I notice something different about the Great Mother…

"You're the one who needs to accept your fate," the Hero declares.

"…Hmm? What are you talking about?"

"Look behind you."

She slowly turns her hardened, creaking neck, then looks behind herself with a curious stare.

"What?!" she yells, and soon, she's at a loss for words.

…It's such a small thing that it's no wonder she didn't notice. I didn't even notice until a few seconds ago. While Ultimate Wall can essentially nullify the damage caused by Seiya's multiple dual-sword strikes, it still doesn't make her immune to impact. After taking constant hits, the Great Mother finds that, little by little, she's been pushed, prodded, and nudged…right to the edge of the Abyss.

"You've grown cautious in your old age? Don't make me laugh. You're three or four meters away from falling into the Abyss and were too stupid to realize it."

While speaking, Seiya vigorously hits her with his dual blades.

"S-stop! S-stop attacking me!"

But Seiya doesn't even pause. I shout to the Great Mother.

"Hurry and lift Elulu's curse! Who knows what'll happen if you fall onto a magic circle powerful enough to turn people into swords!"

"Grrr…!"

The Great Mother ferociously glares at Elulu while slowly backing off the cliff into the Abyss.

"Why?! It makes no sense! Why would you go this far to protect her? She is Igzasion's vessel! She has neither talent nor fighting ability! Without turning into the holy sword, she is worth no more than garbage! She will be of no help to you on your journey! She's garbage!"

"…She isn't garbage."

Seiya's voice is as calm as ever.

"She's my priceless bag carrier."

"Seiya…!"

Tears overflow from Elulu's large eyes. Her little face scrunches up as she sobs.

You could have just said, *She's one of us, and I care about her*, but whatever…

Light Tuchihi   201

Anyway, Seiya, I'm kind of touched! Since when did you start saying such sweet things?!

"Great Mother! Lift the curse, or you're really going to fall!"

"I-i-it's gone! I got rid of it! So stop attacking me!"

Seiya stops his barrage right as her thick feet are one step away from slipping over the edge.

But at the very next moment, she laughs.

"You fool! I got rid of Ultimate Wall, not the curse! Now I can move freely! Trying to kill me is a serious crime! Not even the Hero will be forgiven! You shall suffer my wrath until you cannot even move a muscle! Dragon Breath!"

She opens her mouth wide, exposing her razor-sharp fangs and ravenous flames while she prepares to breathe fire. However, Seiya is already in battle stance in front of her, holding his swords like a cross.

"...Double Wind Blade!"

Swinging his blades like an X, he shoots a sonic wave into the Great Mother's stomach at a tremendous speed, carving a cross into her body before she can even attack. Immediately, she falls off-balance, stumbling back into the Abyss!

Even then, she smiles.

"I have wings! With Ultimate Wall gone, I can finally fly! I shall never fall into the Abyss!"

Moments before falling, she spreads out her wings...only to reveal that one is damaged, filled with holes big enough that I can see the scenery on the other side.

"Wh-what?! My wing...!"

After reaching the realization that she can't fly, her eyes open wide, revealing her enlarged pupils.

"Wh-whyyyyyyyyy?!"

The Great Mother of Dragons's death cry echoes throughout the valley, then through the village.

I imagined I would hear a crash when she hit the bottom. However, even after her screams fade into nothingness and she disappears into the depths of the Abyss, I hear nothing.

"D-don't tell me she's still alive?!"

The curse hasn't been lifted yet! A-at this rate, Elulu…!

The black light is on the verge of making a full circle around her necklace.

"E-Elulu!"

As if the potion has finally worn off, Mash rushes over to Elulu and then…

There's a *click*, and the cursed necklace crumbles to pieces and falls to the ground.

"Ah…"

Elulu rubs her neck in a daze.

"Th-thank goodness…! The Great Mother is gone, and the curse has been lifted!"

Perhaps overcome with emotion, Mash tightly embraces Elulu.

"Elulu! Thank goodness! I'm so glad you're okay!"

"M-Mash, quit it! Y-you're embarrassing me!"

It's just like when Elulu cried and jumped on Mash after the fight with Dark Firus. As I watch over them…

"Phew…"

I'm finally able to breathe a sigh of relief. Then I turn to Seiya, who's casually sheathing his swords.

"Hey, Seiya, can you tell me one thing? How did you damage the queen's wing like that?"

Obviously irritated, Seiya says, "I did it before she used Ultimate Wall. While I used Phoenix Drive to pummel her entire body, I was actually focusing on one of her wings."

"Before she used Ultimate Wall…? B-but that doesn't make sense. I mean, you still didn't know what kind of move that was then, right? So why did you decide to attack one of her wings before that?"

"It was easy to predict she would resort to defending and running away after setting that three-minute time limit on Elulu's cursed necklace. Also, when I used Scan and saw the skill Ultimate Wall, it cemented my suspicions that she'd try to hold out for the next three minutes. Normally, I would have preferred defeating her before she used it, but she had too much HP, making that impossible with what little time I had… That's why I had to get some insurance and take out her only means of escape when backed into a corner, forcing her to remove Ultimate Wall. Her only means of escape, of course, being her wings."

"W-wait. So after your first attack, you were already thinking about what to do after knocking her into the Abyss? J-just how cautious are you?"

"One thing I miscalculated, though, was how her Ultimate Wall was nothing like a wall. I was expecting something closer to the *nurikabe* from Japanese folklore."

"You had no idea what a slime was, yet you know about spirits that manifest as invisible walls…"

"Yes, I know about *nurikabe*. Anyway…"

Seiya stares down into the Abyss with a distant gaze.

"That dragon—how dare she call herself cautious. If you ask me, she was nowhere near cautious enough. If she hadn't waited so long, she could have used Ultimate Wall and kept her wing. Then she could have escaped. If I were her, I would have started using Ultimate Wall during the banquet."

"I-I'm pretty sure it would have been a little too obvious if she started hardening during dinner…"

Just as I'm starting to tire of his absurd predispositions…

"Th-the Great Mother of Dragons fell into the Abyss!"

"This can't be!"

"You bastards! Don't you think you're going to get away with this!"

Dragonewts begin surrounding us, brimming with rage. Some of them are even brandishing weapons. They're clearly out for blood. Even though the Great Mother is gone, we're not out of the woods yet. The dragonewts slowly close in, bloodlust in their eyes. Mash puts himself between Elulu and the mob and draws his sword. Right as I hide behind Seiya, a ray of light shoots up from the Abyss and into the skies.

"Wh-what's going on…?"

As the dragonewts watch with bated breath, a mottled sword with a red-and-black blade rises out of the tunnel of light.

I-is that…?! The Great Mother fell into the magic circle in the Abyss and became the sword!

Seiya naturally grabs the sword and raises it into the air.

"Great. I got Igzasion."

*   *   *

…After a moment of silence, each and every one of the gathered dragonewts unanimously shrieks:

""""That's not Igzasion, you idiot!"""""

I—I can't blame them, though. I mean, Seiya, seriously…?!

I may be dumbfounded, but the dragonewts are enraged.

"That sword's a fake!"

"It doesn't have that legendary sheen!"

"Yeah! Let's kill Elulu!"

"Kill! Kill! Kill! Kill!"

The bloodlust in the air is palpable. However…

"Silence……lizardmen."

With the sword brandished high overhead, the Hero—slayer of the Great Mother—speaks in a well-projected voice, instantly silencing the area.

"Igzasion needs the blood, flesh, and life of a woman of the dragonkin, correct? Well, the Great Mother's life is already in this sword. So…"

Seiya approaches Elulu, then grabs her right arm.

"Ow…!"

Elulu lets out a small cry before a tiny amount of blood trickles down her arm.

"M-Master Seiya…? What are you doing?"

"Get Rista to heal you later."

Seiya picks up the paper-thin piece of flesh with his fingers, then presses it against the mottled sword.

"I will mix Elulu's flesh and blood with this sword."

Perhaps due to using his Synthesis skill, the sword suddenly emits a blinding light and begins to glitter.

The dragonewts are awestruck.

"*Th-there's* the legendary sheen!"

"No doubt about it! Th-that's…!"

"Igzasion! It's Igzasion!!"

Seiya nods in satisfaction before sheathing the blade. Then he says to the dragonewts surrounding us:

"This is perfect. You all were able to fulfill your mission as dragonewts, and I was able to get the holy sword to defeat the Demon Lord. It's a win-win situation for us."

One of the dragonewts mutters, "B-but the Great Mother of Dragons is gone…"

"She became the key to saving the world. Did she not say she would be honored to do so?"

"W-well, I guess…"

"Right? So what's the problem?"

"I dunno. Like…"

"There isn't one. It's a win-win situation."

"A win-win situation… Yeah…"

"Completely win-win. Therefore, the ritual of the holy sword is now over," he clearly states. However, the suddenness of it all only creates commotion, and none of the dragonewts even attempts to move out of the way until…

BOOM!

Suddenly, a loud noise echoes throughout the valley, causing the dragonewts and even me to jump!

After noisily clapping his hands together and getting everyone's attention, Seiya speaks in a voice just as loud as he orders:

"Okay! You can go home now!"

Like children being yelled at by their teacher, the dragonewts hurriedly gather their belongings and trek back down the Dragon Gorge.

CHAPTER 28
Everything's Gonna Be Okay

Using torches to light the way, we quickly follow Seiya down the valley until someone calls out to us from behind. I turn to see the dragonewt Lagos who first led us to the Dragon Village.

"Please hurry to that building. I will send you back to the Dragons' Den."

Lagos appears flustered, but before I can ask him what's wrong, he starts explaining as we walk.

"While you may have obtained Igzasion, there are still many who are unhappy that Lady Elulu survived without becoming the sword. I think you should head back to the continent from whence you came before there's a riot."

"A-a riot?!"

Seiya glares at me as I nervously fidget.

"Is it really that surprising? Their village leader is dead. Of course there would be a riot."

"What happened to the win-win situation you were talking about?!"

"Do you honestly believe they would be content with that? I just used a loud noise and powerful words to temporarily hypnotize them."

"Y-you can even use hypnosis…?"

As fear of the Hero's powers begins stirring within me, Lagos remorsefully regards Mash and Elulu.

"Please forgive my dishonesty. The Great Mother of Dragons told me to say that your families died of illness."

"It's fine. It doesn't matter anymore."

Lagos gives Mash a deep bow.

"Perhaps I have no right to say this, but I am so thankful from the bottom of my heart that Lady Elulu didn't become the sword."

After walking for a while, there are almost no dragonewts around us anymore. A small white house appears at the edge of my vision. That must be where we teleported from the Dragons' Den. When we head inside, Lagos shuts the door. Only after guiding us to the magic circle in the middle of the room does he finally smile.

"Lord Mash, Lady Elulu, this is perhaps the last time we will ever meet. However, I will be praying for prosperous futures for you both. May peace and glory be with you."

They smile back at Lagos.

"Th-thanks, man!"

"Thank you, Lagos!"

"Hero, Goddess, please use Igzasion and save the world."

I thank Lagos in Seiya's place.

...After coming to Dragon Village and meeting everyone, I thought they lacked empathy and emotion for the most part. However, it appears there are good dragonewts like Lagos as well. I'm sure Elulu's and Mash's parents were great people, too.

As Lagos begins casting the spell...

"Wait."

Seiya speaks up. He is holding a small dragonewt—er...a small lizard for some reason.

"I picked it up on the way here. Teleport this first."

Lagos's face twitches.

"A-again...?"

"Just because we got here safely once doesn't mean we can do it twice. Besides, for all I know, you could be the angriest that Elulu is still alive."

"S-Seiya! How rude! Would it kill you to trust someone?!"

However, Lagos simply shakes his head with a serious expression.

"It's fine. Perhaps that level of caution is one of the Hero's strengths. It saved Lady Elulu this time, but one day, it may even save the entire world."

"Uh… Being careful is going to save the world…huh?"

Anyway, I think it's really mature of Lagos not to get angry. I mean, I have no idea how old he is just by looking at him, but yeah.

"I'm really sorry about this. Could we start with the lizard, then?"

After pointlessly teleporting the lizard back and forth *twice*, we're finally able to be teleported to the Dragons' Den ourselves.

After stepping off the magic circle, we find ourselves in a dimly lit, narrow space with bare rock.

"Phew. We're finally back, huh?" I mutter to myself when all of a sudden…

"Seiyaaa!"

Elulu suddenly jumps into Seiya's arms and begins to cry.

"Thank you, thank you, thank you, thank you! I was so scared! I was so scaaared…!"

It appears all her pent-up feelings came bursting out the moment we got back.

"I didn't want to be a sword! I didn't want to die! Because if I died, I wouldn't be able to talk to you all anymore!"

Elulu buries her face in Seiya's stomach and sobs. Just watching her is making me tear up.

"Elulu…! I'm sorry! I'm so sorry! I should have been the one to stop you!"

"It's okay! It's not your fault, Ristie! You're a goddess! You were just prioritizing the entire world instead of one person!"

The Hero gives us a reproachful gaze as we blubber together.

"Stop. You're being loud…and annoying."

He grabs Elulu's head with one hand and peels her off. He then takes her confused, crying face and presses it against Mash's chest. Unlike Seiya, Mash simply holds her in his arms without saying a word. After a few minutes go by, she bashfully offers:

"You know what? When I was told I was gonna be a sword…the hardest thing for me was knowing I'd never be able to talk to you again, Mash."

"M-me too, Elulu. I couldn't bear the thought of losing you."

Splashes of crimson light their cheeks as they gaze into each other's glistening eyes.

What?! H-hold up! Are these two going to start dating or something?!

Love and adventure go hand in hand. Although we shouldn't let them get carried away, I don't think we'll have anything to worry about.

As a goddess—as a woman, I decide to give them some space.

"Mash, Elulu, could you wait for us outside the cave?"

"Huh? Wh-why?"

"I'm sure you two have things to talk about, right? Plus, Seiya and I need to have a little talk as well."

"A-all right, that's cool, I guess."

"Okay! We'll be waiting in front of the cave, then!"

Mash and Elulu hold hands as they walk out of the cave. I watch over them while smiling at Seiya.

"Ugh! They're so innocent—so adorable!"

"Is that why you sent them off together? Ridiculous."

"Hey, I wasn't lying when I said I wanted to talk to you alone."

"I have nothing to discuss with you."

Although we're finally alone together in a narrow space, my smile does a one-eighty as I tightly knit my brows and give Seiya a dirty look.

"About the Dragon Killers you synthesized…you said you pulled the hairs directly out of my head, right?"

"Yes. And?"

"What do you mean, 'and'?! What are you going to do if I go bald?! And I can't believe you sneaked into my room when I was asleep! This is criminal stuff here, you know!"

"If I hadn't had one hundred strands of your hair, then I wouldn't have been able to make the Dragon Killer. You can't blame me for that."

As always, he has a point, but that's not what I wish to discuss.

"…You didn't do anything else, right?"

"What are you talking about?"

"Y-you know… L-like, uh… I'm asking if you took advantage of me while I was sleeping!"

"All I did was pluck one hundred hairs off your head. Nothing else."

R-really?! …Wait. *"All I did was pluck one hundred hairs off your head"*? Is this just a thing people are supposed to be okay with now? Who even says that?! He should be arrested!

Seiya begins to turn on his heel when…

"Seiya! Stop right there! I'm not done with you yet!"

"Tsk. What now?"

I point at the sheath on Seiya's hip, then with a serious expression…

"That sword *isn't Igzasion, is it?*"

Seiya's paying attention now.

"…What did you say?"

Seiya stares at me with a distant, almost chilling look in his eyes. I gulp.

"I-I'm a g-goddess, you know! I admit, that sword is strong! But I don't sense any kind of holy aura from it that's going to help us defeat the Demon Lord!"

After glaring at me with a scary look on his face for a few moments, his expression returns to normal.

"I underestimated you. It seems you're more than a walking health potion."

"I seriously hope that's a joke…"

"You're right, though. This isn't Igzasion. This is a platinum sword-plus that I synthesized."

"I knew it. You used that to fool the dragonewts, huh? To save Elulu…"

"She's my bag carrier. I don't like it when others try to override my decisions. That's all."

Seiya begins to walk before saying, "Listen, this conversation is just between you and me. If the little one hears, she'll start crying and making noise again."

"Y-yeah, I know. I won't say anything."

Following Seiya, I ask:

"Hey, Seiya, what will you do if the Great Mother was right? What if Igzasion is the only way to defeat the Demon Lord?"

"I'll just find another way to defeat him. Didn't you tell the Great Mother that yourself?"

"I—I just said that in the heat of the moment, though… I don't know if there really is another way."

After a few moments of silence, Seiya murmurs…

"Everything's gonna be okay."

"Huh?"

Something feels very off about what he just said. Without giving a reason, without evidence, he just said that everything was going to be okay. That's not the Seiya I know.

"…What's wrong, Rista?"

Seiya's staring at me now, likely because I stopped short without saying anything. His intense gaze makes me gasp.

"N-nothing at all! My head just went blank for a second because you said something out of character!"

"Your empty head went blank? We need to get you to the hospital."

"Who are you calling empty-headed?! I'm not afraid to smack a Hero, you know!"

"Come on—let's go. They're waiting for us."

Seiya looks at the cave exit and squints. A blinding light peeks through the small entrance.

And just like that, we walk forward, slowly heading into the light.

…In the long run, not getting Igzasion is probably going to be a huge pain when it comes to saving this S-ranked world Gaeabrande. However…I'm sure that this Hero—that Seiya—will be able to pull it off. That's what I truly believe in this moment.

After deciding to go forward without looking back, I suddenly feel unbelievably exhausted. So much happened at Dragon Village. Mash, Elulu, and Seiya won't say it, but they must be really tired as well. Maybe we should head back to Izale village's inn and sleep for a day? …Yeah! Let's do that! Sometimes we need to forget about saving the world to rest and relax a little together! I'm never going to forgive him for plucking a hundred hairs off my head while I was sleeping, but he did say something that really made me happy: *I only eat what she makes me.* Tee-hee! Once we're back at the village, I'm going to buy some ingredients and make him a feast! Of course, I'm going to treat Mash and Elulu as well.

But though I walk out of the cave with a spring in my step, what awaits us is less than ideal. A dozen or so armored soldiers surround Mash and Elulu on the rocky expanse by the cave entrance.

"M-master!"

"Ristie!"

Before they can explain, a group of soldiers rushes over to us and takes a knee. When I look closely, I see they have cuts all over their bodies. They're filthy, and the scratches on their armor stand out. They look battle worn.

A soldier struggles to speak. It's as if his exhausted body is being lashed with a whip.

"We are the Roseguard Imperial Knights! We heard that the Hero headed toward this cave, so we immediately came here from Olga Fortress!"

"O-oh… And what would the imperial knights want with us?"

I have an idea of what they want, but I ask just in case. They wear deeply troubled looks.

"Captain Rosalie's imperial knights are currently in battle with the Demon Lord's special forces north-northeast from here! The battle is not going in our favor! Hero, please come with us!"

Their expressions alone tell of the imminent danger.

I give them a smile brimming with the compassion of a goddess.

"All right, let's go."

The soldiers' faces light up. Some even cry. But hidden behind the kindness, I inwardly scream:

Why can't I catch a breeeeeeeeeak?!

The S-ranked world of Gaeabrande doesn't even give us a moment's rest.

AFTERWORD

Nice to meet you. My name is Light Tuchihi. First off, I want to thank you for reading *The Hero Is Overpowered but Overly Cautious*. By the way, do you enjoy RPGs? If you ask me, there are two types of RPG players: those who try to play through the story and don't care about leveling up, and those who grind, get the best weapons and items available, and carefully progress through the game. Just so you know, I'm the latter. I hate being killed by enemies and having to start over, so I like to take my time to grind and prepare. I like to think there are many others who do the same.

The protagonist of this story is also a cautious one. He's just more cautious than most. After being summoned to another world, he makes sure he's as prepared as can be. If you read this story, you know just how obsessed he can get. He's abnormal. The goddess he travels with is sick of it, she complains, and she even gets angry with him from time to time.

There are countless *isekai* anime, manga, and novels right now, but as the author, I can guarantee there are no protagonists as cautious as this one. But he's not just careful. He's strong as well. As a writer, nothing would make me happier than if you enjoyed Seiya Ryuuguuin's humorous behavior, the aggravation he causes the goddess Rista, the trouble Mash and Elulu endure, and the way Seiya utterly destroys powerful enemies through careful and meticulous preparation.

At first glance, Seiya Ryuuguuin may seem rude and selfish, so I think some readers may be turned off by him, but he is caring in his own way and acts accordingly. I would like to go more into that next volume.

By the way, I had Seiya give his catchphrases in English, and a lot of his moves were in English as well, so please come after me about grammar. (lol)

For example, the original English catchphrase I came up with for Seiya is "Ready Perfectly," but that probably sounds weird to a native English speaker. Normally, the Japanese equivalent of this phrase would be "準備は完璧 / Junbi wa Kanpeki," but a native English speaker might say something like "All set."

Therefore, while the English may not be correct, as an author, I'm prioritizing tempo and sound, so please just ignore the weird English.

Now that we're on the subject, the correct counter for deities isn't 人 (people) but 柱 (pillars/gods). However, I decided to count everyone as a person to unify the language. It would just get complicated to have Rista not count herself as a person during conversation. Therefore, please ignore that as well.

…And that's about it. I was trying to give some extra insight into the language used, but I probably just ended up rambling. (lol)

Anyway, finally, I would like to thank everyone who helped me! First off, I would like to thank the illustrator, Saori Toyota! Thank you so much for your beautiful work. I love how cool Seiya turned out; how cute Rista is; and how charming and wonderful Mash, Elulu, and the other characters turned out. Their designs are perfect and just how I imagined them.

Also, I would like to thank everyone who supported me at KakuYomu! This novel was originally written on an Internet novel site called Kaku-Yomu. On that site, everyone can rate and comment on the novels posted, and thanks to all your love and support, this series made it to the bookshelves. Thank you so much.

Next, I would like to thank my editor. There are a lot of things I would have never noticed that could be seen only through the eyes of a reader. Thank you so much. Thanks to sharing opinions and editing together, a lot of the inconsistencies were ironed out, and I am confident this became something anyone could enjoy. I still remember how confused I was when you first sent me the reviewed manuscript on the computer after changing the background color to black. I didn't realize you did it to make it easier to see the corrections made in red. But now I look back fondly on the time I sent you that e-mail saying, "Yo! The manuscript is black?! What's up with that?!"

Now, last but not least, I would like to thank everyone who bought this book! Thank you very much. As the author, nothing would make me happier than to know that the reader—you—laughed, or felt refreshed, or forgot about your day-to-day troubles, or simply thought, *I'm glad I bought this book*. Thank you so much for picking up this novel.

One more thing.

"Everyone! Be like the protagonist of this story and make sure you buy the book, a spare, and another spare for when you lose the spare."

This is what I was planning on saying at first, but then I was worried everyone online would think, *Man, this author's desperate…* So I just want you to know how honestly grateful I am that you bought even one copy. I won't even joke about asking you to buy more copies from now on. (lol)

I don't know. Maybe I'm thinking too much about it. Maybe I'm being overly cautious just like the protagonist of this story?

I was writing this to show my appreciation, but I think I just started rambling again. Anyway, I hope we meet again in the next volume.

Light Tuchihi

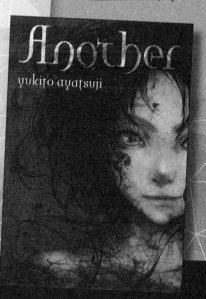